'I'm going to make you mine over and over again, until you don't even know who you are any more.'

Rocco was standing at the window of his bedroom with his back to the view of a faint pink dawn breaking over London's skyline. His arms were crossed and he was looking warily at the woman sleeping in his bed, feeling as if he'd just been catapulted back into reality after a psychedelic mind-altering experience.

Those words were reverberating in his head. When he'd said them to her he'd meant that he wanted to make her forget her own name because she'd made him forget…*everything*. Who he was. What he was. Why he was.

Abby Green got hooked on Mills & Boon® romances while still in her teens, when she stumbled across one belonging to her grandmother in the west of Ireland. After many years of reading them voraciously, she sat down one day and gave it a go herself. Happily, after a few failed attempts, Mills & Boon bought her first manuscript.

Abby works freelance in the film and TV industry, but thankfully the four a.m. starts and the stresses of dealing with recalcitrant actors are becoming more and more infrequent—leaving her more time to write!

She loves to hear from readers, and you can contact her through her website at www.abby-green.com She lives and works in Dublin.

Recent titles by the same author:

THE CALL OF THE DESERT
THE SULTAN'S CHOICE
SECRETS OF THE OASIS
IN CHRISTOFIDES' KEEPING

Did you know these are also available as eBooks?
Visit www.millsandboon.co.uk

THE LEGEND OF DE MARCO

BY
ABBY GREEN

First published in Great Britain 2012
by Mills & Boon, an imprint of Harlequin (UK) Limited.
Harlequin (UK) Limited, Eton House, 18-24 Paradise Road,
Richmond, Surrey TW9 1SR

© Abby Green 2012

ISBN: 978 0 263 89060 0

Harlequin (UK) policy is to use papers that are natural, renewable and recyclable products and made from wood grown in sustainable forests. The logging and manufacturing process conform to the legal environmental regulations of the country of origin.

Printed and bound in Spain
by Blackprint CPI, Barcelona

THE LEGEND OF DE MARCO

This is especially for Haze, you're a doll.
Thanks for being my friend since we were spotty teenagers
with dodgy hair styles. Point Break Forever! x

CHAPTER ONE

ROCCO DE MARCO felt contentment ease into his bones as he took in his surroundings. He was in a beautiful room in a world-renowned museum, right in the heart of cosmopolitan London. It had been designed by a famous French Art Deco designer in the 1920s and drew afficionados from all over the world to see its spectacular stained-glass windows.

The crowd was equally exclusive: high-ranking politicians, erudite commentators, A-list celebrities and billionaire philanthropists who controlled the world's stockmarkets with a flick of a finger or the raising of a brow. *He* was in the latter category, and at the age of thirty-two was surrounded by hushed and awed speculation as to how he'd achieved his untouchable status in such a short space of time.

At that moment he caught the eye of a tall, elegant, patrician blonde across the room. Her glossy hair was pulled back into a classic chignon, and her haughty blue gaze warmed under his look. He did notice, however, that not a tinge of *real* colour came into those carefully rouged cheeks. She was dressed head-to-toe in shimmering black, and he knew that she was as hard as the diamonds at her throat and ears. She smiled and raised her glass to him in a small but significant gesture.

A sense of triumph snaked through Rocco as he raised

his glass in a mirror salute. The prospect of wooing the immaculately bred and oh, so proper Ms Honora Winthrop flowed like delicious nectar through his veins. His gut clenched hard. This moment was *it*. He was finally standing at the pinnacle of everything he'd fought so hard for. Never had he dared to imagine that he would be in such a position—hosting a crowd such as this, contemplating becoming an indelible part of it.

He was finally standing far enough above and away from the degradation of his young life in the slums of a poor Italian city where he'd been little more than a feral child. With no way out. He'd been spat upon in the street by his own father and he'd watched his half-sisters walk past him without a single glance at their own flesh and blood. But he *had* clawed his way out, with guts and determination and his infamous intelligence. And to this day no one knew of his past.

He put his empty glass on the tray of an attentive hovering waiter and declined another one. Keeping his wits about him was as ingrained in him as a tattoo on his skin. For a second he thought of the crude tattoo he'd borne for years, until he'd had it removed. It was one of the first things he'd done on his arrival in London almost fifteen years ago, and his skin prickled now at the uncomfortable reminder.

He shrugged it off and went to stake his claim on Ms Honora Winthrop. For a brief second a sense of claustrophobia rose but he clamped down on the sensation. He was where he wanted to be, where he'd fought to be.

Composing himself, and irritated that he felt the need to do so, he found his eye snagged and caught by a lone figure. A female figure. He could see immediately that she was not half as polished or alluring as the other women in the room. Her dress was ill-fitting and her hair was a long, wild tangle of vibrant red. It suggested that there was something untamed about her, and it called to him on some deep level.

Rocco's mind emptied of its original purpose. He couldn't look away from the enigmatic stranger.

Before he had even registered his intent he'd veered off course and was moving in her direction...

Gracie O'Brien was trying to look nonchalant. As if she was used to being a guest at glittering functions in London's most prestigious venues. When in fact she was more used to being a waitress...in far less salubrious surroundings. The kind of places where men habitually pinched her bottom and said crude things about her lack of ample assets.

She gritted her jaw unconsciously, acknowledging that in today's economic climate a hard-won yet paltry art degree didn't count for much. She had a dream. But unfortunately to finance her dream she needed to work and to eat and survive. And the only jobs available to her right now were on the menial end of the scale.

She mentally shook herself out of the uncharacteristic introspection. She could handle the menial end of the scale. She couldn't handle *this*. She was clutching her bag to her belly. *Where had Steven gone?* She'd only come tonight as a favour to him. Her mouth compressed. Tension gnawed at her in this kind of surroundings—along with the habitual anxiety she felt for Steven.

Gracie forced herself to relax. This annual charity benefit thrown by the company her brother now worked for signified a huge turning point in his life—which had to explain his moody humour and nerves lately. That was all it was. She had to stop worrying about him. They were twenty-four now, and she couldn't go on feeling responsible for him just because she'd taken on that role from as far back as she could remember, when she'd been the one who had inevitably stood between him and some bully. She still bore scars of the scrapes she'd been in, protecting her little brother—younger by twenty fraught minutes.

Their mother, before she'd abandoned them, had never let Gracie forget that her beloved son had almost died, while Gracie had had the temerity to flourish with rude health. Her mother's parting words to Gracie had been, *'I'd take him with me and leave you behind if I could— he's the one I wanted. But he's too attached to you and I can't deal with a screaming brat.'*

Gracie pushed down the surge of emotion she felt whenever she thought of that dark day, and sighed when she finally caught sight of her brother in the distance. Her heart swelled in her chest with love for him. Despite their abandonment, and so much that had happened since then, they'd always looked out for one another. Steven's inherent weakness had meant that even Gracie's strength hadn't saved him for a few dark years, but now he was back on track.

Her brother had implored her earlier, 'Please, Gracie... I really want you there with me. They're all going to have their wives with them. I need to fit in. Do you know what a coup it is to get a job with De Marco International...?'

He'd gone on to wax lyrical once again about the godlike Rocco de Marco. So much so that Gracie had relented just to make him stop rhapsodising about this person who couldn't possibly be human because he sounded so perfect.

She'd also relented because she'd seen how anxious he was, and she knew how hard he'd worked for this chance. Long hours in prison, studying and sitting his A-levels so that he could get into college as soon as he got out. The constant fear that he would relapse back into his old drug-addicted ways. But he hadn't. Finally his uniquely raw talent and intellect was being used.

He was talking to another man. To look at Steven across the room, no one would even think he was related to Gracie. Steven was tall, and as skinny as a rake. Gracie was five foot five and her almost boyish figure caused her no end of dismay. Her brother was blond, pale and blue-eyed. She was red-haired, freckled and brown-eyed, taking after their feckless Irish father. Another reason why her mother had hated her.

She grimaced now, when her dress slipped half an inch further down her chest, exposing even more of her less than impressive cleavage. She'd seen it in a charity shop earlier and hadn't tried it on. *Big mistake*, Gracie grumbled to herself. The dress was at least two sizes too big and trailed around her feet like her nan's dresses had when she'd been a child playing dress-up.

She gave up hope that Steven was coming to look for her, figuring he was too busy, and turned her back on the crowd to hitch up her dress. She faced a buffet table groaning under the weight of platters of deliciously delicate canapés and an idea struck her.

Happily engrossed in her task a few minutes later, she froze when a deep and sexily accented voice drawled from nearby, 'The food won't disappear, you know… Most of the people in this room haven't eaten in years.'

The cynical observation went over Gracie's head. She flushed guiltily, her fingers tightening around the canapé she'd just wrapped in a napkin to put in her bag along with the three others she'd already carefully wrapped up. She glanced to her left, where the voice had come from, and had to lift her eyes up from a snowy-white broad chest, past a black bow tie and up to the most arrestingly gorgeous vision of masculinity she'd ever seen in her life.

The canapé dropped unnoticed from her hand into her open bag. She was utterly gobsmacked and transfixed. Dark eyes glittered out from a face so savagely beautiful that Gracie felt ridiculously like bowing, or doing something equally subservient. And she was *not* a subservient person. Sexual charisma oozed from every unashamedly masculine molecule.

'I...' She couldn't even speak. Silence stretched between them.

One ebony brow went up. 'You...?'

His mouth quirked, and that made things worse because it drew her attention there, and she found herself becoming even more mesmerised by the decadently sexy shape of his lips. There was something so provocatively sensual about his mouth. As if its true purpose was for kissing and only kissing. Anything else would be a waste.

Her face flaming now, because she was not used to thinking about kissing men within seconds of meeting them, Gracie dragged her gaze back up to those black eyes. She was aware that he was tall and almost intimidatingly broad. But it was actually hard to process the reality that the rest of him was equally gorgeous. His hair was thick and black, with one lock curling on his forehead. It gave him a devilish air that only enhanced the strong features which held a slightly haughty regard.

He carried an unmistakable air of propriety, his hands in his pockets with easy insouciance, and that realisation finally managed to dissolve Gracie's paralysis. She contracted inwards, lowered her eyes. 'The food isn't for me... It's for...' She searched wildly for some excuse for her gauche actions and thought belatedly of what Steven would say if she was thrown out for this. Maybe she'd read this man all wrong? She glanced up again and asked suspiciously, 'Are you Security?'

Even as the words left her mouth, and there was a clearly incredulous split second before he threw his head back to laugh throatily, she knew she shouldn't have said anything. This man was no mere security guard.

The sting of embarrassment, the knowledge that she was utterly out of her depth in these surroundings, made Gracie retort sharply, 'There's no need to get hysterical about it. How am I meant to know who you are?'

The man stopped laughing, but his eyes glittered with wicked amusement—further raising Gracie's ire. She knew that she was reacting to the very peculiar effect he was having on her body. She'd never felt like this before. Her skin was sensitive, with goosebumps popping up despite the heat of the room. Her senses were heightened. She could hear her heart thumping and she felt hot—as if her insides were being slowly set on fire.

'You don't know who I am?'

Blatant disbelief was etched into the man's perfect features. Gracie amended that thought. They weren't actually perfect. His nose looked slightly misaligned, as if it had been broken. And there were tiny scars across one cheek. Another faint scar ran from his jaw to his temple on the other side of his face.

She shivered slightly, as if she'd recognised something about this man on a very deep and primal level. As if they shared something. Which was ridiculous. The only thing she shared with a man like this was the air they were currently breathing. His question and his incredulity brought her back to earth.

She hitched up her chin. 'Well, I'm not psychic, and you're not wearing a name tag, so how on earth *should* I know who you are?'

That gorgeous mouth closed and firmed, as if he was trying to keep in a laugh. Absurdly Gracie felt like smacking him and had to curb the flash of he renowned temper, which unfortunately *did* match her hair.

'Who are you, then, if you're so important that every-one should know you?'

He shook his head, any trace of humour suddenly gone. Gracie shivered again, but this time it was because she saw another facet of this fascinating specimen of maleness. Strange how in the space of just mere seconds she felt as if she was seeing hidden layers and depths in a complete stranger. Now he had a speculative gleam in his eyes. She sensed strongly that behind the easy charm lurked some-thing much less benevolent—something dark and calcu-lating.

'Why don't you tell me who *you* are?'

Gracie opened her mouth, but just then a man materi-alised between them and directed himself to the tall man/god, completely ignoring Gracie as if she was some ran-dom nobody—which, she needed no reminding, she was. But also as if he was used to inserting himself between women and this man—which was extremely irritating.

'Mr de Marco, they're ready for you to give your speech.'

Shock slammed into her. *Mr de Marco?* This man she'd just been ogling was Rocco de Marco? From the way Steven had described him and his achievements she'd imagined someone much older. And quite possibly short and fat, with a cigar. Not this dynamic, virile man. She guessed him to be early thirties at the most.

The obsequious man who'd interrupted them melted away, and Rocco de Marco stepped closer to Gracie. Immediately his scent hit her, and it was musky and dis-turbingly masculine. He put out his hand and, still in shock, she lifted hers to let him take it. His eyes never leaving hers, he bent down and pressed a kiss to the back of her small, pale and freckled hand. Inwardly, even as her blood leapt to his touch, she cringed at how work-rough her hands must feel.

He stood again and let her hand go. He wasn't speculative any more. He was all hot and seductive. 'Don't go anywhere, now, will you? You still haven't told me who you are…'

And then after a searing look he turned and strode away into the throng. It was only then that Gracie breathed again. Unable to stop herself, she took in the sheer masculine majesty of his physique. He stood head and shoulders above most of the crowd, who were parting like a veritable Red Sea to let him through. A broad back tapered down to narrow hips and long legs. Physical perfection.

He was Rocco de Marco. Legendary financier and billionaire. Some people called him a genius. Wildly her glance searched for and found Steven, who was looking raptly to where Rocco now stood on a dais, commanding the packed ballroom.

Without even knowing quite why it was so important to get out of there, Gracie just knew she had to leave. The thought of facing that man again was frankly overwhelming. Her utter gaucheness screamed at her. The rough skin on her hands itched. Not one person in that room could be unaware of who he was. Except her. The sheer class of these people struck home—hard. The jewels the women wore were *real*, not like her cheap plastic baubles. She didn't belong here.

She thought of how the most important man in the room had witnessed her filching canapés from the buffet, and when she had a scary vision of being introduced to him by Steven she blanched. Steven would be mortified if Rocco de Marco mentioned it. He might even get into trouble.

That well ingrained sense of responsibility kicked in and
Gracie did the only thing she could do. She ran.

Rocco de Marco regarded the profile about him in the
newspaper's financial supplement with a disdainful twist
of his lips. A cartoon depiction of his face made his features markedly more masculine and dark. A dart of satisfaction ran through him, however, when his eye went to
the picture which had been taken of him with the glacially
beautiful Honora Winthrop. He knew without arrogance
that they looked good together—dark against pale. It had
been taken at the De Marco Benefit in the London Museum
the week before. The night he'd embarked on his campaign
to seduce his way into respectable society for ever.

His smile turned hard at the thought of how eager Ms
Winthrop had been to get into his bed. But so far he'd re-
sisted her lures. He'd made the decision that night that the
endgame would be to make her his wife, and in pursuing
that aim he wouldn't allow sex to cloud the issue. His smile
faded when he conceded that it hadn't taken much effort
on his part to resist her.

As if to taunt him, the image of a petite, sparky redhead
inserted itself mischievously into his mind's eye. It was so
vivid that it drove him up and out of his chair. He stood at
the vast window of his office which overlooked London.
The view went as unnoticed as the paper which had fallen
to the floor with his abrupt move. Rocco's jaw clenched
in utter rejection of that image and memory. And the extremely uncomfortable reminder that after his speech he'd
not gone straight to Honora Winthrop's side but to look
for the nameless stranger—only to find that she'd disappeared.

He could still remember his shock and surprise. No
one—especially not a woman—walked away from him.

He didn't relish the fact that not once before in the fifteen years since he'd left Italy had he ever deviated from his well-laid plans—not even for a beautiful woman. She hadn't even been that beautiful. But she'd been *something*. She'd exerted some kind of visceral pull on him the moment he'd seen her across the room.

For that entire evening he hadn't quite been able to stop his reflex to look for her. It burned him to acknowledge that he was still thinking of those few seconds of what should have been an unremarkable meeting. Especially when he was on track to achieving the stamp of respectability which would forever put him in a sphere far, far away from his past.

In an uncharacteristic gesture of fatigue Rocco rubbed the back of his neck. He put his momentary introspection down to the recent security breach in his company. It had been quickly discovered and sealed off, but had made Rocco realise how dangerously complacent he was becoming.

He'd hired Steven Murray a month ago—as much on a gut instinct as anything else, which was not normal practice for him. But he'd been unusually impressed with the young man's raw eagerness and undoubted intellect, and something about the man had connected with Rocco on a deep level. So, despite the worryingly vague CV, Rocco had given him a chance.

Only to be rewarded just this past week by the same man transferring one million euros to an unlocatable account and disappearing into thin air. The party last week had been a high point—and now this. It was like a punch in the face to Rocco. A sharp reminder that he could never let his guard down for a second.

His skin went clammy when he thought of how the people he sought so desperately to be his peers would turn their backs on him in a second if he revealed himself to be vulnerable in any way. And if that happened how quickly Honora Winthrop's gaze would turn disdainful if he even dared ask for her hand in marriage.

For so long now he'd been in absolute control, and suddenly he was chatting up random women in ill-fitting dresses and hiring people on gut instinct. He was in danger of jeopardising everything he'd worked so hard to attain. He was courted and fêted now because wealth made him powerful. It would be social acceptance that would secure his position for ever.

This chink in his otherwise solid armour made him wary. People were already curious about his past. He didn't want to give the hungry English tabloids any excuses to dig even further.

The fact that his security team had failed to find Steven Murray yet was like an irritating splinter stuck in Rocco's foot. He would not rest until the man had been found and questioned. And punished.

With a grimace at his own moody thoughts, Rocco turned from the view and picked up his jacket to leave his glass-walled office. Dusk was enveloping the city outside and the offices surrounding him were empty. It was usually his favourite time to work—when everyone had left. He liked the enveloping silence. It comforted him; it was so far removed from the constant cacaphony of his youth.

Just as he was almost out of his office the phone rang. Rocco turned back and picked it up. He heard what the person on the other end said and his whole body tautened. He bit out his words. 'Send her up to me.'

Tension kept Rocco's body tight as he walked to his lift and watched the numbers ascend. Someone was here asking for Steven Murray. There was a pause when the lift stopped, and in the split second before the doors opened

Rocco had a prickling sensation of something momentous about to happen.

The doors opened to reveal the petite form of a woman dressed in a grey T-shirt, faded jeans, and what looked like a cardigan tied around her waist. Her form was lithe and compact, with small pert breasts pushing against the fabric of her top. A heavy coil of red hair lay over one shoulder, reaching almost to those breasts. Her face was pale and heart-shaped, her freckles stood out, and her eyes were huge and brown, flecked with gold and green.

Instant recognition, shock, and something much hotter slammed into Rocco as he reached in and clamped his hands around slim arms almost as if he had to touch her before doing anything else.

He breathed out incredulously. *'You!'*

CHAPTER TWO

'You…' Gracie echoed faintly, still reeling after the lift doors had opened to reveal…*him*. In a haze she asked, 'What are you doing here?'

Rocco de Marco's hands pulled her from the lift, forcing her legs to move and she heard the faint swish of the doors closing again behind her. Her heart was thumping, and shock choked her at being faced with this man again.

His hands were on her arms like vices. 'I own this building,' he ground out, dark eyes blazing down into hers. 'I think the more pertinent question is this: why are *you* here, looking for Steven Murray?'

Dimly Gracie realised that he recognised her from that night they'd met a week ago. But there was no comfort in that. Adrenalin was pumping through her at seeing Rocco de Marco again, but from one look at his face she could take a wild guess and assume Steven was far away from this place. And in big trouble.

She couldn't speak. She could only look up into the most arrestingly handsome features she'd ever seen for the second time in just over a week.

His grip tightened. '*Why* are you here?'

Gracie shook her head, as if that might force oxygen to her malfunctioning brain. 'I just… I thought he might be here. I wanted to find him.'

Rocco's mouth tightened into a flat line. 'I think it's safe to assume that Steven Murray is in any number of locations now—none of which are close to here if he's got half a brain cell. He's done what most criminals do: they go underground.'

Gracie's heart stuttered at hearing her own fears so baldly spoken, but her innate protectiveness surged upwards even as her conscience protested. 'He's not a criminal.'

One of Rocco's brows arched up. 'No? Then what would *you* call stealing a million euros?'

If Rocco de Marco hadn't been holding her arms then Gracie would have fallen down. *A million euros?*

'What is he to you? Your lover?' He almost spat the words out.

Gracie shook her head and tried to back away—a futile exercise while he still held her arms. Paramount was the need to protect Steven at all costs as she tried to assimilate this mind-boggling information.

'I'm just worried about him. I thought he might be here.'

De Marco all but snorted. 'He's hardly likely to return to the scene of the crime. I don't think he's stupid enough to try and steal another million from the same source.'

Gracie felt trapped and claustrophobic, but fire surged up. 'He's not stupid!'

With a desperate wrench to get away that had more to do with this man's intensely physical effect on her than anything else, Gracie finally freed herself from his hands and whirled around, wildly searching for escape. She spotted emergency doors in the distance and sprinted, hearing a faint curse behind her. Just as her hands were about to touch the bar her shoulders were caught and she was twirled around, landing with a heavy thud against the doors. Rocco de Marco was glaring down into her face, hands either side of her head, effectively trapping her.

On some rational level Gracie knew she shouldn't have run, but the shock of hearing what her brother had done was too much. She realised now that she'd just made herself look as guilty as Steven.

As if reading her mind, Rocco de Marco breathed out and said in a chilling voice, 'You're obviously in this too—up to your pretty neck. The question is: why did you come back here? It must have been to get something important.'

She shook her head, her anger fading as fast as it had risen and leaving her feeling sick. 'Mr de Marco, I swear I'm not involved. I'm just worried. I came because I thought Steven might be here. I don't know anything.'

His face grew even harder and it sent a shiver through Gracie.

'You knew who I was last week when we met.'

It wasn't a question. She shook her head again. There was a quivery feeling in her belly at the thought of that meeting now. 'No...I didn't. I had no idea. Until that man came and used your name.'

As if not even listening to her, Rocco de Marco said, 'You were there with Murray as his accomplice. You and he cooked the whole thing up.'

Gracie just shook her head. It was throbbing with a mixture of anxiety and lingering shock. Rocco de Marco's focus seemed to come back to her, and with something that sounded like a snarl he stood up straight and took her arm, ignoring her wince. He was frogmarching her back to the lift and Gracie panicked, having visions of police waiting for her downstairs.

She started to struggle. 'Wait... Look, please, Mr de Marco, I can explain...'

He cast her a dark look as he punched a button on the lift. 'That's exactly what you're going to do.'

Fear and trepidation silenced Gracie as he pushed her into the lift ahead of him, yet kept a hold on her arm, and pressed another button once they were in. Silence, thick and tense, swirled around them, and Gracie cursed herself for coming here in the first place.

Standing next to him in the lift, she had a very real and physical sense of the disparity in their sizes. Her head barely grazed the top of his arm. His tautly muscled strength radiated outwards, enveloping her in heat. Gone was any trace of the man who had oozed warmth and seduction the night they'd met. Evidently if you moved within his rarefied milieu you were accorded his attention. A few steps out of it, however, and it was an entirely different story.

Gracie did not need this situation to demonstrate to her that someone like Rocco de Marco would look right through her if he saw her in her natural habitat. Her stomach twisted. She'd faced down many opponents over the years with plucky resilience, but for the first time she recognised someone who was immovable. And more powerful than anyone she'd ever encountered.

Oh, Steven, she groaned inwardly. *Why did you do this?*

He'd rung her earlier, and she could still taste the acrid fear in her mouth when he'd said, 'Gracie, don't ask any questions—just listen. Something has happened. Something really bad. I'm in serious trouble so I have to go away…'

She'd heard indistinct noises in the background, and Steven had sounded distracted.

'Look, I'm going away and don't know when I'll be able to get in touch again. So don't try and call, okay? I'll e-mail or something when I can…'

Gracie had clutched the phone with sweaty hands. 'Steven, wait—what is it? Maybe it's something I can help you with…?'

Her heart had nearly broken when he'd said, 'No. I won't keep doing this to you. You've done enough. It's not your problem, it's mine—'

Gracie had cut in, with fear constricting her voice. 'Is it…drugs again?'

Steven had laughed, and it had sounded a little hysterical. 'No…it's not drugs, Gracie. To be honest, it might be better if it was. It's work… Something to do with work.'

Before she'd been able to ask him anything else he'd said goodbye and cut her off. She'd kept calling his phone but it had only answered with an automated message to say that it was out of service. With a sick feeling she could well imagine he'd chucked his phone. She'd gone round to the small, spartan bedsit that he'd been so proud of and found it trashed, his stuff everywhere. No sign of him. And then she'd remembered him mentioning work and so she'd come here, to De Marco International, to see if by some miracle he was sitting in his office.

But she hadn't even got that far. The minute she'd seen Rocco de Marco's face she'd known her brother was in serious trouble.

Gracie was so preoccupied that it was a moment before she realised they'd ascended and she was being walked out of the elevator and into what looked like a penthouse apartment. The stunning dusky views over London added a surreal touch to the events unfolding.

A huge full moon was rising in the beautiful bruise-coloured sky, but it went unnoticed as Rocco let her go and moved about, switching on lights which sent out pools of inviting warmth. Gracie shivered and rubbed her arms.

The rush of adrenalin and shock had dissipated, leaving her feeling drained.

She looked around and was surprised to notice that the penthouse, for all its modernity, exuded warmth and an understated opulence. The parquet floor added an antique feel, and the heavy dark furniture stood out against the more industrial architecture, somehow working despite the apparent incongruity. Huge oriental rugs softened the austere lines.

If she hadn't been in such dire straits the artist in her would have longed to explore this tantalising glimpse into Rocco de Marco. Her eyes snagged on his powerful form as he bent and stretched. Her insides twisted and tightened—who was she kidding? Her interest in this man stemmed from a much more carnal place than an interest in aesthetics.

Rocco rounded on the petite woman who now stood in his apartment and curbed his physical response to that pale freckled skin and the wild russet hair which still trailed over one shoulder to rest on the curve of one small breast. The wild look in her eyes just before she'd sprinted away from him downstairs was burnt into his memory. It had touched something deep inside him. A memory. And he'd lost precious seconds while he'd been distracted.

She was nothing like the soignée beauties he usually favoured. Women renowned for their breeding, looks, intellect and discretion. Women who wouldn't have allowed him to lay a finger on them if they knew what kind of world he'd been born into.

Anger at his own indiscriminate response and something much deeper—a dark emotion which seethed in his gut as he thought of her as Steven Murray's lover—made him say harshly, 'You will tell me everything. Right here and now.'

When she flinched minutely, as if he'd struck her, he ruthlessly clamped down on the spike of remorse. She looked very pale and vulnerable all of a sudden. Rocco chastised himself. She was no quivering female. There was an inherent strength about her that warned of a toughness only bred from the streets. He recognised it well, and he didn't like to be reminded of it.

He dragged out a nearby chair and all but pushed her into it. Her small heart-shaped face was turned up to him and his insides tightened. *Dio*, but she was temptation incarnate with those huge brown eyes and those soft pink lips. Displaying a kind of artful innocence. His instinctive reversion to Italian even in his head just for that moment surprised him. He'd spent long years doing his best to erase any trace of his heritage. His accent was the one thing that proved as stubborn as a stain, reminding him every time he opened his mouth of his past. But he'd learnt to embrace that constant reminder.

There was a long, tense silence, and Rocco tried to figure out what was going on behind her wide eyes. And then she looked as if she was steeling herself for a blow. 'What did you mean when you said Steven stole a million euros?'

Rocco opened his mouth and was about to answer when he stopped. Incredulous, he said, 'You have the temerity to *still* pretend ignorance?'

He saw her small hands clench to fists on her lap. He remembered how spiky she'd been with him that night at the benefit, and how intrigued he'd been by her. He remembered kissing her hand, the feel of slightly rough palms which had been so at odds with the soft skin of the women he was used to, and how it had sent a dark thrill though him. She must have known exactly who he'd been and *they* must have been laughing at him all week. He burned inside. He hadn't felt so uselessly humiliated in years.

She'd seen him in a weak moment and he didn't like it. At all. He hadn't been weak since he'd left Italy far behind him, with its stench-filled slums and the humiliation he'd endured. Thinking of that restored Rocco's fast unravelling sense of control. With icy clarity he said, 'Who are you, and how do you know Steven?'

Gracie glared balefully at Rocco de Marco. He had the uncanny ability to make her feel as if you had no option but to comply with his demands. The man was like a laser.

'Well?'

The word throbbed with clear frustration and irritation. He was standing in front of her, hands on hips. His shoulders were broad under the white shirt, tapering down to lean hips. In the dim light he was like some beautiful dark lord. Heavy black brows over deepset pools of black. High cheekbones. A strong nose with that slight misalignment. And those lips…full and sensual. The lock of hair she remembered still curled on his forehead, but even that didn't soften the taut energy directed her way.

Half without thinking Gracie said, 'I'm Gracie. Gracie O'Brien.'

His mouth took on a disdainful curve. 'And? Your relationship to Steven Murray?'

Gracie swallowed. She was afraid if Rocco de Marco knew she and Steven were related he would expect her to know where he was for sure. She could feel the blush rising even as she formulated the words. She'd never been able to lie to save her life. 'He's…he's an old friend.'

Rocco's eyes went to her mouth and he said mockingly, with a chill kind of menace, 'Liar.'

Gracie shook her head. Protecting her twin brother was

so ingrained she couldn't fight it. And didn't want to. He'd protected her over the years as much as she'd protected him. Just in a different way. 'That's all he is. An old friend. We go back…a long way.'

Rocco's mouth twisted and disgust etched his features into a grimace. 'You go back to a double bed in a squat somewhere.'

Gracie paled at the very thought. Bile rose. She shook her head more strongly. 'No. *No.*' She stopped short of saying *That's disgusting*, and closed her mouth. 'Really… it's not like that.' She'd half risen out of the chair and her hand was out, as if that could reinforce her words. She sat back down abruptly.

Rocco folded his arms across his chest, but that only brought her attention to the awesome strength in his arms, the bunched muscles. She felt curiously light-headed all of a sudden, but put it down to the fact that she hadn't eaten all day.

'I'll tell you what it's *like*, shall I?' Rocco didn't wait for her to answer. 'You're Steven Murray's accomplice, and both of you were stupid enough to think that you could come back to the scene of the crime to recover something important. What was it?' he continued. 'A flash drive? That's the only thing small enough to have escaped our searches.'

Before she knew what was happening Rocco was right in front of her, hauling her out of the chair. Amidst her confusion and shock Gracie was aware of the fact that his touch on her arms was light, almost gentle this time. The contrast of that touch to the fierce energy crackling around them made her even more confused. But he was squatting at her feet now, running big hands up her legs.

It took a second for the fact to register that he was frisking her. His hands were now creeping up the insides of her legs. She reacted violently, jerking away, hands slapping everywhere, catching Rocco's silky head. He cursed and stood up, catching hold of her arms again with his hands. This time he wasn't gentle.

'You little wildcat. Hold still.'

Holding her captive with one hand, he quickly delved into her pockets with his free one and turned them out. The speed with which he moved made Gracie feel dizzy. Soon she was standing there with the linings of pockets sticking out and the disconcerting feeling of his hands probing close to her skin.

This time when she jerked back he let go, and she almost stumbled. She felt violated—but not in the way she should have. It was in some illicitly thrilling way.

'You...' she spluttered. 'I'd prefer to be dragged down to the police station than have your hands mauling me.' A sudden realisation sliced through the frantic pulse in her blood and she asked faintly, '*Have* you called the police?'

Rocco stood back. His face was flushed. With anger, Gracie had to assume, not liking the way her blood pooled heavily between her legs even as she struggled to concentrate. He had gone very still.

He shook his head and with clear reluctance admitted, 'I haven't called the police because I don't want the news that I employed a rogue trader to get out. It could ruin my reputation. Image and trust are everything in this game. If my clients knew I'd jeopardised their precious investments I'd be finished within days as rumour and innuendo spread.'

For a second Gracie felt nothing but abject relief flowing into her veins, but the cruel smile on Rocco's face made her blood run cold again.

'Don't assume for one second that not calling the police gives your lover a reprieve. Do you think an overworked police force or a fraud squad can be bothered looking for one man?' He shook his head and crossed his arms. 'I have people looking for Steven right now, and they have infinitely more sophisticated resources at their disposal. It's only a matter of time.'

Fear constricted Gracie. 'What'll happen to him?'

Rocco's face was hard. '*After* he's returned every cent of the money? Then I will blacklist him from every financial institution in the world and hand him over to the fraud squad whilst protecting my own anonymity. He could be looking at ten years in jail. I have used my own money to bridge the gap caused by his stolen funds. He owes me personally now.'

Gracie felt weak. She groped to find the chair behind her and sat down heavily. Her brother would never survive another day in jail. He'd told her fervently when he'd got out that he would prefer to die than end up there again.

Rocco frowned. For the first time this evening he could swear the woman in front of him wasn't acting. She looked like a car crash victim. He had to resist the urge to ask if she wanted a drink.

She was looking at the ground. Not at him. Rocco wanted to go to her and tip her chin up. He didn't like how disconcerted he felt not being able to look into her eyes. And then she did look up, and her eyes were like two huge dark pools, made even darker against the sudden pallor of her skin.

She opened her mouth. He could see her throat work. She shook her head and finally said, 'I can't... I can't lie to you. This is too serious. I haven't told you the truth about Steven.'

Rocco felt the hardness return. He ruthlessly pushed down the weakness which had invaded him for a moment.

'I'm getting bored waiting for it. You have one minute to speak or I *will* hand you over to the police as an accomplice and deal with the consequences.'

Gracie's head was too tangled up with fear and shock for her even to try and persist in making Rocco de Marco believe she wasn't related to Steven. His casual mention of jail had decimated her defences completely. Any faint hope she'd been clinging onto that there must be some kind of mistake had also gone. Gracie knew with a defeated feeling that Steven wouldn't have run if it wasn't true. He must have been trying to play for stakes way outside his league. Was that why he'd gone for the job in the first—?

'*Gracie!*'

Her feverish thoughts stuttered to a stop and she looked up at Rocco. Her name on his lips did funny things to her insides. For a moment she'd forgotten she was under his intense scrutiny. Illicit heat snaked through her abdomen, and in the midst of her turmoil she couldn't believe he was affecting her so easily.

Taking a deep breath, she stood up, her legs wobbling slightly. 'Steven is not my lover and I'm not his accomplice... He's my brother.'

'*Go on.*'

Rocco's voice could have sliced through steel. He'd crossed his arms again and her gaze skittered over those bunched muscles.

Gracie shrugged minutely, unaware of how huge her eyes looked in her small face.

'That's it. He's my brother and I'm worried about him. I was looking for him.' She wasn't sure why, but she didn't want to let Rocco know that he was her *twin* brother. That information suddenly felt very intimate.

Rocco's jaw clenched, and then he said slowly, 'You

expect me to believe that? After everything I've just witnessed and after I saw you at the benefit last week? You were both cooking up this plan together.'

Gracie shook her head. 'No. It wasn't like that, I swear. I only went with Steven because—' She stopped. She couldn't explain about her brother's inherent insecurity and how badly he needed to fit in. And also she'd realised now why he'd been so abnormally anxious for the past few weeks—way more than she would have expected for new job nerves. She felt sick.

Rocco filled in the silence, 'Because you and he had a grand plan to do some inside trading and make yourselves a million euros without anyone noticing.' He emitted a curt laugh. 'For God's sake, you couldn't even help yourself stealing food from the buffet!'

Gracie flushed bright red. 'I took that food for my next-door neighbour. She's old and Polish, and always talks about when she used to be rich and go to balls in Poland. I thought they would be a nice treat for her.'

This time Rocco did laugh out loud, head thrown back, exposing his strong throat. Gracie burned with humiliation, her disadvantaged upbringing stinging like an invisible tattoo on her skin.

Rocco finally stopped laughing and speared her with those dark eyes again. Gracie fought not to let him see how much he affected her. It scared her, because ever since her mother had left them, and then their nan had turned her back on them, leaving them to the mercy of Social Services, Gracie had allowed very few people close enough to affect her—apart from her brother.

Becoming slightly desperate, she flung out a hand. 'I barely passed my O-level Maths. I wouldn't know a stock from a share if it jumped up and bit me. Steven is the smart one.'

'And yet,' Rocco went on with relentless precision, 'you were with him last week, flaunting yourself in front of me. You *knew* who I was.'

Gracie sucked in an outraged breath that had a lot to do with the memory of how transfixed she'd been by him that night. 'I was *not* flaunting myself. *You* came over to *me*.'

At this Rocco de Marco flushed a dull red, and for the first time Gracie had a sense that she'd gained a point. But any sign of discomfiture was quickly erased and his face became a bland mask again. Bland, but simmering—if that was possible.

Quickly, before he could launch another attack, Gracie admitted reluctantly, 'I was with Steven because he was self-conscious about going alone.'

Rocco's lip curled. 'I have yet to believe that you are even Steven Murray's sister. Why does he have a different surname?'

Gracie shifted uncomfortably and knew she must look pathetically guilty. She looked down. 'Because…because he fell out with our father and took our mother's maiden name.' It wasn't entirely untrue.

'Not to mention the fact that you look nothing like him.'

Gracie looked up to see Rocco's dark gaze travelling up her body, over her chest to her face. She could feel the heat rising. 'No,' she snapped. 'I know I look nothing like him. But not all—' She stopped abruptly, realising she'd been about to say *twins*. She amended it. 'Not all families resemble each other. He looks like my mother and I look like my father.'

She crossed her arms too, feeling ridiculously defensive, and knew it was only because for her whole life she'd wondered if she'd looked more like their mother would she have loved her the way she'd loved Steven? Would she have stayed?

The fact that she'd eventually abandoned them both was little comfort and a constant source of guilt for Gracie. She could still remember the long nights of hugging her brother as he'd cried himself to sleep, wondering where their mother had gone.

For a long time she'd felt it had been *her* fault, because her mother hadn't wanted her. It was only with age and maturity that she'd realised their mother had had no intention of ever taking Steven—too wrapped up in her own problems and her own dismal world.

After a long moment of glaring at Rocco, Gracie could feel herself sway. Her vision blurred slightly at the edges. Just as she was inwardly cursing her own weakness Rocco emitted something unintelligible and came towards her, putting a big hand on one arm. She stiffened at his touch, hating the incendiary effect he had on her, but at the same time aware of how close she was to collapsing. Like some Victorian heroine in a swoon. *Pathetic.*

She tried to pull away, but to no avail.

Rocco said, from far too close, 'When was the last time you ate, you silly woman?'

This time she did pull free, and glared at him again. 'I'm *not* a silly woman. I've just been…worried. I didn't think about eating.'

That black gaze swept up and down again and his lip curled. 'You don't seem to think about eating a lot.'

He strode away from her and Gracie watched him, half mesmerised by his sheer athletic grace. He flung over his shoulder. 'There are some instant meals in the fridge. Follow me.'

Gracie felt seriously woozy now. Rocco de Marco was offering her *food*?

She tore her gaze away from six feet four of hard-muscled alpha male and looked to the apartment entrance, beyond which lay the private lift doors. Suddenly the distance to freedom seemed tantalisingly close.

As if he'd read her mind Rocco materialised again a few feet away, with hands on his hips, and said softly, 'Don't even think about it. You wouldn't make it to the next floor before you were returned.'

Her heart stammered as she looked at him. 'But…I didn't see anyone.'

Rocco winked at her, but there was no humour on his face. 'Haven't you watched any Italian movies? My men are everywhere.'

Gracie tried to reassure herself that he was just joking, but she had the very real sense that if she did try to leave some faceless person *would* materialise and frogmarch her back to Rocco. She knew enough from the streets to know when someone meant business. And Rocco de Marco meant business. She was as captive as if he'd tied her to a chair.

He turned to walk away again and with the utmost reluctance, and yet an illicit excitement fizzing in her blood, she followed him.

It was only when Rocco was pressing the button on the microwave oven that a cold wave of realisation washed over him. What was he *doing*? Feeding the enemy? All because for a moment she'd looked as if she might faint at his feet? Her face had been so pale that it had sent a shard of panic through him, and as much as he wanted to deny it he had to admit that her shock had been almost palpable. And yet every instinct he possessed counselled him not to trust his judgement in this. He'd learnt early how women could manipulate. He'd seen his mother manipulate her way through life right up until she died.

Closing his eyes for a moment, Rocco willed the image away. His hands clenched on the countertop as he heard Gracie come into the kitchen behind him. Why the hell was he even thinking of that now?

He schooled his features and turned around. Something suspiciously like relief went through him when he saw that her cheeks were a bit pinker. Her big eyes were darting around the vast room and he welcomed the surge of cynicism. No doubt she was already calculating the worth of everything. That was what he would have done. Years ago. Before figuring out what he could take.

The microwave pinged and he turned to take out the ready meal, finding a plate and some cutlery. He all but threw it down in front of her, then gestured to a stool and growled out, 'You're my only link to Steven Murray, and if you're going to lead me to him then I don't want you fainting away.'

Her eyes flashed at that, and her mouth tightened as if she was about to refuse the food. A shaft of desire he couldn't control made Rocco clench his hands to fists. He hated her for his arbitrary response.

'Go on. Eat.'

CHAPTER THREE

GRACIE chafed at Rocco de Marco's high-handedness. She hitched up her chin and tried to ignore the tantalising smell of food. Even that alone was making her feel weak again with hunger.

'Are you going to leave it in front of me until I eat it? Like an autocratic parent?'

Rocco leaned forward on the other side of the counter and Gracie fought not to move back. 'I'm no parent and I'm no autocrat. Just eat.'

Gracie looked down to escape that blistering gaze and saw creamy mashed potato and what looked like succulent beef pieces in a stew of vegetables. This was no standard ready meal—this was from a fancy deli. Her stomach rumbled and she went puce.

Defiant to the end, even as she gave in and pulled back the covering she said waspishly, 'I might have been vegetarian, you know.'

She heard a noise that sounded slightly strangled, but wouldn't look at Rocco for fear of what she might see. She started transferring the food onto the plate, hating being under his watch but too hungry to stop.

After a moment he said, with over-studied politeness, 'Forgive me for not checking with you first.'

She cast him a quick glance and something in her belly

swooped. He'd been laughing at her. She hurriedly looked away again and concentrated on the food. Once the first succulent morsel of beef hit her mouth she was lost, and devoured the lot like a pauper who hadn't eaten in weeks.

From out of nowhere a napkin and a glass of water materialised. Gracie wiped her mouth and took a long drink of water. Only then did she dare to look at Rocco again. He was staring at her, transfixed. She immediately felt self-conscious and wiped her mouth again. 'What? Have I got food somewhere?'

He shook his head. His voice sounded rough. 'When was the last time you ate?'

For a moment Gracie couldn't actually recall. She fidgeted with the plate and mumbled, 'Yesterday…lunchtime.' But in fact she knew she hadn't really eaten properly in days.

'Where do you live?'

Gracie met Rocco's dark and hard gaze. Something in his demeanour had changed. He was back into questioning mode. And then the full reality of her situation flooded back. She flushed and avoided his eyes. She felt like such a pathetic failure at that moment.

'Gracie…' he said warningly, and her insides flipped again at the way he said her name. It felt incredibly intimate.

She looked at him and squared her shoulders. She couldn't go any lower in his estimation, and perhaps if he knew just how harmless she was he'd let her go?

'I lived in Bethnal Green until this morning. But I lost my job two days ago and they wouldn't give me my wages. I couldn't give my landlord the full rent today, so he suggested I make it up to him in other ways.'

Gracie shuddered reflexively when she remembered his sweaty face, grabbing hands and acrid breath. Before she knew it Rocco had moved. She felt her right hand being picked up and he was inspecting the grazed and reddened knuckles. She'd forgotten, and winced slightly because they were still tender.

He speared her with a glance, 'You hit him?'

She shrugged slightly, more mortified than ever now. She hated her instinct to fight. She'd had it ever since someone had picked on Steven when they'd been tiny. 'He was backing me into a corner. I couldn't get out.'

Still holding her hand, Rocco said grimly, 'I suppose I should consider myself lucky you didn't aim a swing at me too.'

Gracie looked up at his hard jaw and figured she would have broken her hand if she had. He was standing very close now, still cradling her hand. Her belly clenched and a coil of something hot seemed to stretch from her breasts right down to between her legs. And as if on cue she felt a throb, a pulse coming to life.

She pulled her hand away and started babbling. 'I left my cases at Victoria train station in the left luggage. I should go and get them and find somewhere for the night.'

She was off the stool and backing away now, as if she'd forgotten for a moment why she was there in the first place, suddenly terrified at the weak longing that had sprung up inside her when Rocco had held her hand.

He continued to just look at her with his arms folded. 'I told you before that you won't make it to the next floor if you try to leave.'

Panic rose up, constricting Gracie's voice. 'You can't keep me here. That would be kidnap. I only came to Steven's office to try and find him. That's *all*. I really don't have an ulterior motive. I didn't take anything and I didn't know about the money.'

Rocco looked at the woman in front of him. Strange

how his entire world had contracted down to her since he'd seen her in the lift. For a second that knowledge threatened to blast something open inside him, but Rocco reminded himself that she was providing him with the key to finding the culprit who'd had the temerity to think he could take advantage of him.

That was why he hadn't thought about anything else.

It had nothing to do with the fact that just a moment ago, when he'd held her hand in his and seen her bruised knuckles, he'd felt rage within him at the thought of some faceless man threatening her.

To divert his mind away from those provocative thoughts, he asked, 'Why did you lose your job?'

He could see her hands ball into fists. She was like a glorious feline animal, bristling and lashing out in defence, and a curious weakness invaded his chest. When he'd watched her eating ravenously he'd been mesmerised—first of all because he wasn't used to seeing women eat like that, and also because it had reminded him of *him*. He would never forget what it was to be hungry.

'I had issues with some of the customers.'

Rocco arched a brow and welcomed being forced to refocus on the present. 'Customers?'

She flushed pink. 'I worked in a bar in a less than salubrious part of town.' And then she said in a rush, 'Just temporarily.'

Again Rocco felt a kind of rage growing within him—not at her, but *for* her. He could well imagine men finding her feisty allure something to challenge and harness. She was proving to be altogether far more of an enigma than she'd appeared that night just a week ago.

Out of nowhere, immediate and incendiary, Rocco had the desire to see her tamed and acquiescent, and he wanted to be the one to tame her. Sheer shock at the strength of that desire made Rocco blanch for a moment. Women like her should hold no appeal for him. It felt like a self-betrayal. Before she could see anything of his loss of composure, and wondering if he'd lost his mind completely, he strode forward and stopped in front of her, as if to prove to himself that he *could* stand in front of her and restrain himself from tipping her over his shoulder like some caveman. The surreal circumstances of their meeting and her connection to Steven Murray was causing this completely uncharacteristic response, that was all.

As implacable as a stone wall, he told her now, 'You're not leaving this apartment until your brother—' He broke off and swore for a moment. 'If he even *is* your brother, is found and brought to task for his actions. Now, give me the ticket for your bags and I'll have them picked up.'

Scant minutes later Gracie found herself being shown into a sumptuously decorated guest bedroom. She still wasn't entirely sure how she'd allowed herself to be bulldozed into submission, but on some very secret level she felt so tired. For the first time in her life she was being subservient to someone else and she couldn't drum up the energy to fight it. She had no one to turn to and nowhere to go—literally. An uncharacteristic wave of loneliness washed over her.

'There's a bathroom through there, with a robe and toiletries. When your bags come I'll bring them to you.'

Gracie looked around with wide eyes gritty with fatigue. Rocco was striding towards the door and she envied his seemingly unstoppable force. If she'd known there was a chance she might bump into him again there was no way she would have ever attempted to go to her brother's office. She sighed. Too late for regrets now.

Rocco turned at the door, filling it with his broad frame. 'We'll discuss where we go from here in the morning.'

Some sliver of fight sparked within her. 'You'll let me walk out of this apartment. Because if you don't—'

He cut her off. 'You'll what? Call the police?' He shook his head and smiled with insufferable coolness. 'No, I don't think so. I'm sure you don't want the police sniffing around your brother any more than I want the news leaked that I employed an inside trader.'

Silence grew and thickened between them. What could she say to refute that? He was absolutely right, and for deeper reasons than he even knew.

He inclined his head in a false gesture of civility. 'Until the morning, Miss O'Brien.'

The door closed softly behind him and Gracie almost expected to hear a key turning in the lock, but she heard nothing. Experimenting, she went to the door and opened it softly. She nearly jumped three feet in the air when she saw Rocco lounging against the wall outside.

'Don't make me lock the door, because I will.'

Wanting to avoid any further questioning or scrutiny Gracie closed the door again hurriedly. She moved like an automaton to the window and looked out over the spectacular view, seeing nothing but her inward turmoil.

It had always been her and Steven—even when their mother had still been with them. And then when their nan had taken them in until she'd declared she couldn't handle two children and had given them over to Social Services.

Their bond had been forged early, when their mercurial mother had cossetted Steven and treated Gracie harshly. One evening, when Gracie had been sent to bed with no dinner for some minor misdemeanour, Steven had crawled in beside her with some food which he'd hidden for her. They'd been four years old.

Steven had always been a target for bullies with his weedy, sickly frame and his thick glasses, so Gracie had got used to stepping in with raised fists. He'd been preternaturally bright, and Gracie knew now if they'd grown up in different circumstances he might well have been nurtured as a genius student. As it was he'd constantly been ahead of his classmates, and yet had patiently and laboriously helped Gracie through the torture of maths and science.

It was thanks to him she'd managed to scrape enough marks in her exams for art college. Even whilst he'd been in the midst of drug addiction and had given up studying himself he'd still been advanced enough to help her. Her belly clenched now when she thought of how Steven had protected her from far worse things than inexplicable maths.

She leant her forehead against the cool glass, and even though her mind was churning with sick worry for her brother she couldn't get another face out of her head. A dark, compelling face with eyes so intense she shivered even now. And she couldn't stop a wave of heat from spreading outwards from her core, threatening the cool distance she'd protected herself with for so long.

Rocco looked at the two battered bags that had been delivered a short time before. One was a backpack and the other an old-fashioned suitcase. The kind you might see in a movie from the 1940s about immigrants leaving Europe for America. She'd left her flat with just *these*? Rocco was used to women travelling with an entire set of matching luggage, complete with personally monogrammed initials. But then he didn't need reminding that *this* woman was a world away from the ones he knew. He shook his head and picked up the bags. He'd long ago given up on the notion of sleeping tonight.

Opening the door to the guest bedroom silently, Rocco

half expected to see Gracie standing on the other side, as obstinate and defiant as ever, but she wasn't. In the gloom his eyes quickly picked out a shape on the bed. Standing still for a moment, he registered she was fast asleep.

Putting down the bags, he felt compelled to go closer. Gracie was lying on top of the covers in a white robe. She was curled up in the foetal position, legs tucked under themselves, hands under her chin. Her hair flowed out around her head like something out of a Pre-Raphaelite painting, the curls long and wild.

Everything in him went still when her head moved and she said brokenly, *'No, Steven...you can't...please...'*

That brought Rocco down to earth with a bang. Once again it was as if she'd exerted some kind of spell over him, making him forget for a moment who she was and why she was here. She was a thieving, lying nobody and her brother had had the temerity to think he could abuse Rocco de Marco's trust.

Rocco stepped back and away from the curled-up shape on the bed, and ruthlessly clamped down on any tendrils of concern or unwelcome desire. He vowed there and then that he would not let her go until he was satisfied that she *and* Steven Murray had been brought to justice.

When Gracie woke in the morning she had the awful sensation of not knowing where she was or what day it was. Her surroundings were completely unfamiliar and scarily luxurious. She was lying on top of a massive bed, in a robe. Slowly, it all came back. Leaving her awful damp flat after nearly being mauled by her landlord, getting that worrying phone call from Steven, and then coming to his office to see if he might be there.

And then she remembered coming face to face with Rocco de Marco. Gracie groaned and put a pillow over her face. *Rocco de Marco*. Her stomach cramped at the vivid memory of his hands around her arms, the way they'd felt when he'd frisked her. The intense excitement in her blood at seeing him again.

Groaning even more, she sat up and saw that the curtains were still open. She now had the most jaw-dropping views out over London, with the Thames snaking like a brown coil through the grey and steel buildings.

She turned away from the view and something caught her eye. She saw her two battered bags just inside the bedroom door. Her face grew hot when she thought of Rocco coming in while she lay sleeping.

Feeling seriously at a disadvantage, Gracie scrambled out of bed and dragged the bags over. She pulled out some jeans and a T-shirt and found her sneakers. After washing her face she dragged her hair back into a knot at the back of her head and left the room.

The entire apartment was still and quiet. Gracie checked her watch. It was still early. Maybe Rocco wasn't up yet? But even as she thought that she got to the doorway of the enormous kitchen and saw him sitting at a large chrome kitchen table. Her heart stopped. He was reading the distinctively pink *Financial Times*. His hair was damp and slicked back from that strong profile. Skin gleaming dark olive in the morning light. Immaculately dressed in a light blue shirt and royal blue tie.

And then he looked up, after taking a lazy sip from a small cup which should have looked ridiculous in his huge hand but didn't. 'Good morning.'

'Good morning,' she echoed faintly, for all the world as if she'd been some benign overnight guest and not one step away from being locked in her room.

Rocco gestured with a hand to the kitchen. 'I'm afraid

you'll have to help yourself. I'm currently without a house-keeper.'

Gracie tore her eyes away from his raw masculine appeal and helped herself to some coffee and toast, which was already laid out. She hated that her hands were shaking. Very little had ever intimidated her, but this did.

She stood awkwardly at the huge island in the middle of the room until Rocco said, a little impatiently, 'Come and sit down. I won't bite.'

Gracie gritted her teeth and reluctantly picked up her coffee and plate and sat down at the other end of the table. She didn't miss his sardonic look. She felt very pale and washed out next to his vibrant masculinity.

She swallowed her toast with an effort and wiped away some crumbs, studiously avoiding Rocco's eyes, and nearly jumped out of her skin when he said, 'I spent a little time investigating your brother last night, and the full picture is very interesting.'

Gracie went cold inside and put down her cup. Frantically she rewound events in her head and froze. She'd told Rocco Steven's real name by revealing her own. She looked at him with wide eyes.

Rocco looked almost bored, but she could sense the underlying anger as tangibly as if he'd started shouting. 'He's got quite an impressive rap sheet. Three years in jail for carrying Class A drugs. Not to mention the fact that he forged papers to get a job in my company so we couldn't find out about his past. His crimes are mounting, Gracie.'

Feeling desperate, Gracie blurted out, 'He's not like that. He really was trying to make a fresh start, to use his intelligence and turn his life around. He did a degree. There has to be some good reason for what he's done—he wouldn't have risked jail again.'

Rocco was impossibly grim. 'I think a lot of people

would agree that a million euros provides quite a good reason.'

Gracie sagged back into her chair and looked down at her pale hands. They were trembling and she clasped them together. Hot tears pricked at the back of her eyes. Rocco's mention of the astronomical sum of money struck hard. She'd almost forgotten about it with everything else that had happened. How could Steven ever come back from this? He'd spend his whole life paying it back. And that was if he was lucky enough to get the chance.

She heard Rocco sigh but couldn't look up, terrified he'd see her emotion. He said with palpable reluctance, 'Nevertheless, I don't think you're about to phone him and tell him to give himself up?'

Willing the emotion down, Gracie looked up. Huskily she admitted, 'I did speak to him yesterday, but he wouldn't tell me where he was, or where he was going, and when I tried to call him back his phone was switched off. I think he's thrown it away.' She omitted to mention that he'd said he'd try to contact her when he could. Gracie vowed then that if that happened she'd tell Steven to stay away and never come back…

Rocco stood up and held out a hand. 'Give me your phone.'

Gracie's mouth opened and closed. Feeling bullish now, she said, 'Why?'

Rocco's mouth tightened. 'Because I don't believe you. Because I think you'll make every attempt to get in touch with your brother and warn him to stay away. And because if he does try and contact you then we'll have him.'

Gracie crossed her arms.

They glared at each other for long seconds and then Rocco bit out with evident distaste, 'Don't make me search you again.'

Something pierced Gracie at the thought of how he'd touched her the night before and how it had obviously repulsed him. In a bid to cover up her emotion she stood up, knowing that he would just find her phone anyway.

She stalked out of the kitchen and retrieved her phone from her bag and brought it back to Rocco, handing it over with a baleful glare. 'He won't call me again. He knows he's in trouble.'

Rocco pocketed the phone and then said casually, 'I have a proposition for you.'

Gracie blinked. She was fairly certain that any proposition from him would be more like a royal decree. Unconsciously she took a step back and could breathe easier. She missed the way Rocco's eyes flashed at her movement.

'I don't have a housekeeper at the moment. I need one.' He flicked a faintly contemptuous glance up and down Gracie's casual clothes. 'I don't see how you could mess up such a basic job. You wouldn't even have to cook. I have a chef who prepares food when I need it. You'd just have to clean and manage the apartment. Deliveries, etc.'

Gracie was struggling to take this in. 'You're…offering me a job?'

Rocco grimaced slightly. 'Well, it's not so much a job as something to keep you busy while you're here. Because you're not leaving my sight until we have your brother.'

Gracie's heart palpitated in her chest at the thought of spending more time with this man. She crossed her arms. 'You can't do this. It's outrageous. You can't just keep me prisoner.'

Rocco arched a mocking brow. 'You have nowhere to go and no job. You've got a grand total of fifty pounds. You're hardly in a position to assert your independence

or freedom. I think you'll find I'm doing you a favour—
which you certainly don't deserve.'

Gracie gasped. 'You looked through my things.'

Rocco shrugged slightly. 'Of course I did.'

Gracie felt ashamed to have her pitiful amount of money
laid out between them like this. She actually had slightly
more than that in a bank account, but it was paltry. Since
she'd finished her art degree she'd been struggling just
to survive, never mind follow her dreams and ambitions.
Rocco de Marco had most likely never even known what
it was like to have to eke out a living.

Forcing herself to not crumble, she said caustically, 'So
you're offering me this *job* out of the goodness of your
heart?'

He smiled, but it was completely without humour.
'Something like that, yes. You're really in no position to
argue, Gracie. You and your brother have got yourselves
into this situation. Look at it this way: you're worth a million euros of collateral until your brother turns up.'

Her mind frantically searched for a way out, but right
then she couldn't see one. She was well and truly trapped.
As much as *she* was the link to Steven for this man, *he*
was her last tangible link to Steven. And there was no way
she was going to leave her brother to face this man's wrath
alone when they did find him.

Gracie straightened her spine and drew herself up, determined to regain some measure of control amidst this
awful powerlessness. 'If I'm going to be your housekeeper
then I want the same amount that I was being paid in the
bar. I have to keep my student loan repayments up.'

Rocco crushed down his surprise at her visible decision
to stay without a fight and tried to ignore the prickling of
his conscience. If she was guilty wouldn't she be doing
her best to persuade him to let her go so she could meet

her brother? And, also, why would she have been stupid enough to come where Steven worked? Rocco crushed the questions. She was up to something—probably just acting this way so that he *would* doubt her guilt.

Curious despite himself, he asked tightly how much she'd been paid and waited for her to triple the amount, which he had no intention of paying. Not with a million euros missing.

Gracie mentioned a figure and Rocco had to stop his shock from registering on his face. Her expression was so guileless and innocently defiant that he found himself inexplicably agreeing to pay her the pathetic sum, and had to wonder if that was even the minimum wage.

Gracie watched as Rocco pulled pen and paper out of a drawer and scrawled a couple of numbers and names on it before putting it into her numb hand.

'That's my executive assistant's number if you need to get me. I'll be in meetings all day on the other side of the city. You can use the phones in the apartment.' His eyes flashed. 'Needless to say, any calls to your brother will be recorded. I've also written down my old housekeeper's number, so you can call to consult with her on what I'll expect.'

Gracie looked down at the paper and then heard his mocking voice.

'My main head of security is positioned right outside this apartment and he can see every movement in and out of the building. If you attempt to leave you'll merely be brought back.'

She looked back and held up the paper, muttering caustically, 'You mean I don't have a direct line to God?'

Rocco smiled and it was wicked, making Gracie's heart-rate and body temperature soar.

'I reserve my private number for people I wish to speak to—not miscreants and thieves.'

His words had an instant effect on Gracie, causing a hot flush of anger to rise when she thought of the long struggle she and her brother had faced to drag themselves out of their adverse circumstances. 'You know nothing about me. *Nothing.*'

His eyes turned cool. 'I know all I need to know. Keep out of trouble until I see you again.'

Gracie watched as he turned and strode away, and shamingly her anger drained away as she found herself wondering what kind of person someone like Rocco would want to give his private number to and speak with in low, intimate tones.

Anger at her wayward imagination made her call defiantly after him, 'Don't think you can get away with this. You're nothing but an…autocratic megalomaniac.'

Rocco turned around and Gracie's heart stuttered to a halt when she saw the anger on his face. Fear gripped her, but it was fear because of her helpless physical response to him. This awful weak yearning he effortlessly precipitated.

'If you're so concerned then by all means call the police. And while you're onto them you can fill them in on your brother's recent activities. I'm sure they'll be delighted to hear about his progress in the real world since prison.'

Gracie gulped. She felt sick. 'You know I can't do that.'

In that moment Gracie could see the long lineage of aristocratic forebears stamped onto Rocco's arrogant features. He had her all boxed up and judged and right where he wanted her.

'Well, then, you'd better get acquainted with this apartment—because it's your home for the forseeable future.'

After he'd walked out Gracie tried hard to drum up

anger or even hatred, but to her intense chagrin all she could seem to think of was the way he'd insisted on feeding her the previous evening.

CHAPTER FOUR

Rocco sat in the back of his chauffeur-driven car. The London traffic was at a standstill. He could sense the tension in his driver and leaned forward to say, 'Don't sweat it, Emilio. I'm not too bothered about time.'

The driver's shoulders visibly slumped a little. 'Thanks, Boss.'

It was only when Rocco sat back again and flicked the switch to raise the privacy window that he went very still. He never usually went out of his way to put people at ease. He thrived on knowing that people never knew what to expect from him, or which way he'd jump. He was never rude to employees. He was scrupulously fair and polite. But he knew he possessed that edge. People were never entirely comfortable around him.

Except for Gracie O'Brien. She wasn't comfortable around him either, but she stood up to him like no one else ever had.

With the utmost reluctance Rocco had to concede that there was a strong possibility she wasn't lying when she said that she'd had nothing to do with her brother's plans. She'd looked far too shocked the previous evening when he'd mentioned jail, and if she'd known what he'd done she'd have to have been aware that jail was an option. Plus there was the fact she'd come to the offices in the first place.

Nevertheless, he'd learnt a lesson about trusting his instincts when it had come to her brother, so he'd be a fool to trust her for a second. Even if everything else had checked out once she'd told him who her brother was.

His security contacts had access to confidential information. She was listed as his sister, no criminal record—unlike her brother. No other siblings. No mention of parents. A grandmother appeared to have brought them up briefly and then Social Services had taken over. They'd come from one of the roughest parts of London, and without even knowing the details Rocco could close his eyes and imagine the scene. Disadvantaged areas were the same the world over.

Going through her pitiful personal possessions, he'd come across a file full of sketches and text. It looked like a mock-up of a children's book and he had to admit it was surprisingly good.

He'd also come across a photo of what had to be her and her brother when they were kids. She'd been freckle-faced, with a huge gap-toothed grin, red hair in pigtails, her arm tight around her smaller brother, who had looked skinny and nervous, shy behind thick glasses.

Rocco felt his chest grow tight. His fists clenched. He would *not* let those huge brown eyes get to him. Or her apparent vulnerability. She was as tough as nails. Clearly out to protect her brother at all costs, whatever her involvement. He'd never really known what that kind of loyalty was like and didn't like the sensation of envy which lanced him. It was further evidence of their bond, and he would watch her like a hawk until her brother resurfaced.

Rocco would not admit on any level that this desire to keep her close had anything to do with her enigmatic personality or her physical appeal. This was about seeing justice meted out. That was all. One million euros of it.

It was only when he looked at the leafy suburbs passing by outside the car that Rocco realised he hadn't thought of Honora Winthrop once. Determined not to let the arrival of Gracie O'Brien derail his life any more than she already had, Rocco made a call and ignored the sense of claustrophobia that spiked when Honora Winthrop answered her phone.

Gracie woke from a fitful sleep at five the next morning. She was still disorientated at first, and a familiar knot came into her belly when she realised where she was. A grey dawn light was breaking over London. Her mind went over the previous day and evening. Thankfully she'd been in bed by the time Rocco had come home, and she'd only heard faint sounds as he'd moved around.

He'd made a curt phone call late in the evening to inform her that he'd be dining out and she'd made a face at the phone, hating herself for wondering who he was dining with. After Rocco had left the apartment that previous morning Gracie had looked wistfully at the apartment door and had even opened it—only to find a large atrium outside and a huge barrel of a man sitting at a desk which seemed to have a dozen monitors.

He'd stood up to an alarming height and asked easily, 'Need to go somewhere, Ms O'Brien?'

Gracie had shook her head. 'I was just having a look around.'

Perfectly friendly, the man-giant had said, 'I'm George, and I'm here to take you wherever you want to go, so if you need anything just shout.'

Gracie had mumbled something incoherent. Evidently George was also there to make sure she didn't go anywhere without him as her close companion. Exactly as Rocco had warned. She'd gone back into the apartment and made a phone call to the last housekeeper, who sounded like a pleasant older woman. She'd cheerfully outlined for Gracie the list of chores Mr de Marco would expect to be done.

Gracie had stood in Rocco's bedroom and looked at the tousled sheets. His unmistakable scent had hung tantalisingly in the air. Musky and male. The indentation caused by his body had been evident, and Gracie had gone hot when she'd found herself wondering if he slept naked.

Feeling hot all over again, thinking of that bed and those sheets, Gracie registered that she was thirsty and got up. She stumbled out of the room, still foggy with sleep.

She was only belatedly aware that the kitchen light was on when she walked in and had to squint her eyes against it. When she saw a big dark shape move she screamed, suddenly wide awake.

Eyes huge, she took in the sight that greeted her. Rocco de Marco was standing in the kitchen, bare-chested and in nothing but a low-slung and very precarious-looking towel, which hugged his hips and barely covered his thighs.

A million things hit Gracie at once, along with a shot of pure adrenalin: he must have just showered as his hair was still damp; his skin gleamed olive in the light; his chest was broad and leanly muscled with a light covering of crisp dark hair that tapered down to that towel in a tantalising silky line.

He was more beautiful than any man had a right to be.

Realising all of those things, and also that she was looking at Rocco as if she'd never seen a man before, she tore her gaze away and blurted out, 'You're meant to be asleep.'

'Well,' he pointed out dryly, 'I'm not. I always get up around now.'

Gracie refused to look at him, hovering in the doorway.

Her heart was still hammering from the shock. 'Shouldn't you…put on some clothes or something?'

Again with that dry voice he pointed out, 'You're equally undressed. I might ask the same of you but I'm not sure I want to.'

At that Gracie looked at him, and felt scorching heat climb up her chest to her face. Rocco's gaze was dark and lazy, taking in her bare legs, the T-shirt which came to the top of her thighs, and then moving back up to her face. Gracie knew she must look a sight, with her hair all over the place and wild. She couldn't for a moment dwell on the fact that she might have seen a predatory gleam in *his* eyes. She could remember the distaste on his face when he'd stood back from frisking her.

Her throat was so dry, but she fought the urge to swallow. It made her voice sound rough. 'I just wanted to get some water.'

Rocco gestured with a hand. 'By all means. Never let it be said that I deny my prisoners the basics.'

That sardonic delivery restored some of Gracie's composure and she willed herself to move forward to the shelves. Very aware of her bare feet and Rocco's lazy gaze, she ignored him and reached up to get a glass on a shelf far too close to him for comfort. And then…couldn't reach it. Not even on tiptoes. She was very aware of her T-shirt riding up over her bottom and cursed silently, thinking of her very worn plain white knickers.

Suddenly a wave of heat emanated from behind her, along with a distinctive scent, and a very muscled brown arm was reaching up past her to pluck a glass down. His front was almost touching her back. Gracie knew if she stepped back she'd walk right into him, and felt weak at the strength of longing that rushed through her to know what it would feel like to have his arms wrap around her.

But then he put the glass down on the counter beside her with a clatter and moved away, taking that heat with him. Gracie gripped the glass and slowly turned around. For a big man he moved incredibly silently and gracefully. He was already on the other side of the kitchen island, sipping from a mug, regarding her as coolly as ever.

Gracie felt as if she was wading through treacle just getting to the sink to pour the water. The air had become dense with some kind of tension that was completely alien to her. She felt as if it was coiling deep within her, making her feel alternately light-headed and shaky.

'There's bottled water in the fridge.'

Gracie filled the glass and cursed herself for not going that route in the first place. 'Tap water is fine. Bottled water is a waste of money.' She turned around with her glass clutched in both hands like a shield.

Rocco raised a brow. 'Now you're an environmentalist?'

Pride stiffened Gracie's backbone. 'I do care about the environment, as it happens.'

Before he could question her again, or make some acerbic comment, he put his cup down. 'If you'll excuse me I've got a busy day ahead.'

He moved towards the door with all the lethal grace of a jungle cat, and yet looked as suave as if he was fully dressed. Gracie's eyes felt burnt just from looking at all that bared skin and taut musculature.

He turned at the door and said with a definite glint in his eye, 'Remind me to show you how to do hospital corners. That's how I prefer my bed to be made in the future.'

She looked at the empty door after he'd disappeared and it took a few seconds for his words to register. When they did, she wanted to throw the glass into the empty space he'd left behind. The arrogant so and so. She clamped her lips tight together. She would *not* let him get to her. She repeated this to herself as she went back to her bedroom, feeling very skittish.

Rocco stood under the punishing spray of a cold shower just a few moments later. Damn that woman. When she'd appeared in the doorway in nothing but that flimsy T-shirt and bare legs he'd blinked because he'd thought she was an apparition. He'd only just had a shower which he'd had to turn to cold because he'd woken from lurid dreams of stripping Gracie O'Brien bare and laying her out on his bed in all her pale glory.

When he'd realised she wasn't an apparition the blood had rushed south and hardened his body with an embarrassingly immediate effect. Thankfully she'd been so shocked to see him he didn't think she'd noticed.

He'd been unable to compose himself, as if confronted with a naked woman for the first time. He cursed volubly. What was it about her that turned him on so effortlessly? She was wild and untamed. As unsophisticated as you could get. Freckles, for crying out loud. All over. All down her legs and arms. And, he imagined, on her breasts, which would be so pale against his skin...

He cursed again when he thought of her stretching up to get that glass. His eyes had glued to her smooth pale thighs and the pert curve of her bottom, that tantalising glimpse of white cotton. Never had such an unsexy fabric looked so sensual. Like a fool he'd moved closer, ostensibly to help her reach the glass, only to come so close that he had been able to smell the surprisingly sweet and clean scent of her shampoo. No perfume, just something faint, like wild flowers. More subtle and alluring than he would have imagined possible.

Her hair had brushed his bare chest and the nearly overwhelming urge to press close and slide his hands up and under that shirt, around to cup her breasts and feel their weight and firmness, had had him jumping back and away like a scalded cat to the other side of the kitchen.

Rocco shut off the shower and stepped out for the second time in the space of half an hour. He vowed at that moment to do everything in his power to find Steven Murray, so that he could draw a line under this incident once and for all and get this woman out of his head.

For two days Gracie managed to avoid Rocco by making sure she was up after him in the mornings and in bed before he came back to the apartment at night. Luckily, he seemed to be busy. She was congratulating herself on having evaded him for the third morning in a row when he suddenly emerged from the study in the apartment, issuing a string of expletives, looking seriously disgruntled. And absolutely gorgeous in faded jeans and a T-shirt.

Gracie couldn't avoid bumping straight into him, and sprang back as if burnt, heat washing through her body like a tidal wave. She went hot and cold all at once. She could smell his scent on the air, musky and masculine. He glowered at her from his superior height and Gracie fought the urge to apologise.

To fill the silence and deflect him from her embarrassment she blurted out, 'What are you doing here?'

Looking seriously disgruntled now, he said, 'Sometimes I work from this office—if that's all right with you?'

A little redundantly she found herself asking, 'Is there something wrong?'

Rocco's dark gaze swept over her and Gracie burnt up even more.

'My chef has just rung to say he's ill, and his replacement is busy. I have someone coming for dinner this evening and I didn't want to go out, but now it looks as though I'll have to.' Rocco chafed at having to look at the reasons why he *didn't* relish being seen out in public with Honora Winthrop, when just a few days ago he would have welcomed the prospect. The woman standing in front of him, who'd been avoiding him zealously for the past two days, was far too close to those reasons for comfort.

Something pierced Gracie's insides as she wondered churlishly if this dinner was a date. His mistress, perhaps? Again, almost without thinking, she found herself saying, 'I can cook if you like?'

Rocco smiled mockingly. 'You? Cook?'

His obvious incredulity combined with her recent disturbing flash of something which felt awfully like jealousy made her say waspishly, 'I can do better than baked beans and toast, if that's what your tastes run to.'

His eyes darkened at that, and dropped again in a leisurely appraisal, as if he was contemplating his tastes running to *her*. Gracie squirmed. He was just playing with her.

She drew back and stepped away, feeling seriously prickly, cursing herself and her mouth. 'Look, forget I said anything. It was a stupid idea.'

She was almost past him when he caught her arm and stopped her. His entire hand wrapped around her bicep. The breath stopped in her throat and she swallowed painfully. Slowly, she turned and looked up. His expression was contemplative, and he didn't let her go.

'Can you really cook?'

Gracie nodded, and fought the urge to tug her arm free. She didn't want him to see that he affected her. 'If you give me a list of what you want I'll do my best. How many is it for?'

A shadow crossed his face. He dropped her arm abruptly, as if he'd just realised he was still holding it.

'Two.'

That curious pain lanced Gracie again. She crossed her arms. 'I can manage two.'

He just looked at her for a long silent moment, until Gracie felt like screaming with tension, and then he nodded slowly. 'Okay, then. I'll give you the list and we'll eat at eight—after champagne and canapés.'

Later that morning Gracie and George were returning to Rocco's building after a visit to the shops. Rocco had issued her with a credit card and a list of dietary requirements not long after their exchange outside his study.

She'd scanned it and said faintly, 'I'm not sure I can get mercury-free fish from Hawaii at such short notice. Is there anything you're *not* allergic to?'

Rocco had grimaced faintly. 'They're not my requirements. I can eat anything. They're my guest's.'

'Oh.' Gracie hadn't asked who his guest was. She'd just put the piece of paper down and smiled sweetly. 'I'll do my best to work within these narrow parameters.'

To her shock Rocco had looked as if he was holding back a laugh and she'd felt weak inside. But then the look had faded, and he'd just made some inarticulate sound and said, 'Fine. See what you can do.'

It was only as she and George were about to enter the private entrance which led up to Rocco's apartment that Gracie noticed the newspaper headline on the news kisok near them. Her feet stopped in their tracks when she read: *'De Marco to wed society beauty Honora Winthrop...'*

George saw her captivated by the headline and informed her, 'That's the boss's latest companion.'

'You mean his fiancée,' Gracie corrected faintly. She didn't know why, but she suddenly felt flat.

George murmured something else that Gracie didn't hear, and then he was ushering her back into the building as the first few drops of a summer shower started to fall.

At the same moment on a floor high above them, back in his glass-walled office, Rocco was looking at the same headline. This was it. Another milestone moment on the way to securing his position in society. And yet the moment was curiously hollow and empty. He felt constricted, and he loosened his tie and opened the top button of his shirt without even being aware he was doing it.

All he could think about was Gracie's face that morning, when she'd commented about the absurd menu requirements for dinner. He'd wanted to burst out laughing, sharing her moment of incredulity.

No one made him laugh.

It had taken all his control not to pull her up into his arms and plunder that soft pink mouth. To make her close those far too wary brown eyes. To forget everything but *him*.

She'd taken him by surprise, offering to cook dinner. In truth he almost hadn't even registered what she'd said at first, he'd been so busy drinking her in. Not seeing her for the past two days had begun to seriously irritate him, and he'd only realised then that his decision to work from his study had stemmed in part from the fact she wouldn't be able to avoid him in the apartment.

His thwarted desire to see her had also been at the root of his irrational anger over the mere unavailability of his chefs, which would never normally have caused him to flip out.

He could still feel the electrifying sensation of her petite form crashing into him. Arousal had been immediate and burning. His skin had prickled with desire as she'd stood there with that determined chin tilted, daring him to let her cook dinner when he'd been sceptical.

Something outside caught his eye then, and across the expanse of his office space he saw that his private lift was in use, the light ascending. It was probably just George or one of the other bodyguards, but even so his skin tingled. *It could be Gracie.* Before he knew what he was doing he had dumped the paper and was out of his chair, striding to the lift.

Gracie was standing beside George in the lift, still trying to figure out why the news that Rocco was engaged could be affecting her so much. She hardly knew the man, so how on earth could she be feeling…betrayed? He at worst hated her, and at best felt nothing for her. And yet she couldn't help feeling that something intangible had drawn them together besides her brother. She couldn't forget the heated intensity in his eyes the night they'd met.

Or earlier…in the apartment.

Gracie frowned, feeling seriously confused. The lift came to a halt too soon and she looked at George, who just shrugged. They weren't at the penthouse level yet. The doors opened to reveal Rocco standing there, hands on hips. Jacket off, tie loose and top button open. Immediately Gracie's throat went dry and her heart beat faster.

'We were just shopping for dinner,' she blurted out. Why did she feel so guilty when he must know exactly where they'd been?

Rocco looked at George and took Gracie's bags out of her hands, handing them to the huge man whose hands were already full. 'Gracie will be up shortly. I have something to discuss with her first.'

Rocco led the way through a labyrinth of glass-walled offices and Gracie followed reluctantly, still feeling a little raw. She couldn't believe now that she'd ever had the temerity to think she could just waltz into this building to see if Steven might be here. That night felt like an age ago.

Rocco was holding open the door to his office, waiting for her to precede him. Somehow that small chivalrous gesture made her feel even more vulnerable. Once she'd walked in she went into attack mode to disguise her feelings, turning to face him as he shut the door.

'If you're going to have a go at me just because we went to the shops then—'

Rocco put up a hand. 'Have I said a word?'

Gracie shut her mouth and shook her head. She felt very shabby next to Rocco. He'd changed since this morning into a suit. Gracie watched warily as he went around his desk and sat down. And then she took in the full majesty of the awe-inspiring view.

Momentarily distracted despite herself, she went towards the window. 'Do you always have the best views?'

Rocco's voice was cynical. 'Of course. Don't you know that people are judged by how high they are and how far they can see?'

For some reason his words made Gracie feel sad for him. She ran a hand over the back of the sleekly modern chair that faced his desk and returned her gaze to him. 'I wonder when it becomes impossible to be too high, or see too far.'

The weight of silence that stretched between them became almost unbearable and Gracie looked away, feeling embarrassed. Where had *that* little philosophical observation come from?

To avoid Rocco's black gaze she took in the sleek furnishings and modern art that hung suspended on steel wires against the clear windows. Other staff, undoubtedly the best at what they did, were visible through the glass walls of their own offices nearby, but no one was looking up. They were all too busy. Making millions for Rocco and his clients, Gracie surmised grimly. Her brother had been one of those employees and yet he'd stolen from the people who trusted Rocco with their money. Her insides twisted.

She looked back to Rocco and didn't want him to guess the direction of her thoughts. She hunted for something—anything—to say. 'Don't you mind?'

'Mind what?'

Gracie gestured with a hand. 'That everyone can see you? You've no privacy?'

'This office is soundproofed, so no one can hear my private conversations. And this way I can see everyone.'

Gracie looked at him and his face was a bland mask, no expression. It made her feel prickly, wanting a reaction. 'You mean, that way you can control everything.'

Rocco shrugged minutely. 'I couldn't control your brother's scheming to swindle money from me and my clients.'

Gracie looked down and clasped her hands together. He'd just articulated her own thoughts. She heard Rocco move and glanced up to see him standing at his window with his back to her, hands in his pockets. For a moment his powerful physique looked completely incongruous against the cityscape, as if he should be outside, battling something elemental and natural.

He turned then, so abruptly that he caught her staring, and Gracie blushed.

'I hope you're not lying about your ability to cook dinner. I won't stand for any attempt at insolence, Gracie. Tonight is important to me.'

Pain lanced Gracie and she spoke before she could censor herself. 'Because you're entertaining your fiancée?'

Rocco frowned. 'How do you know about that?'

If she could have swallowed her own tongue she would have, but she said miserably, 'I saw a headline outside.'

For a long moment Rocco just looked at her, and then said, 'She is not my fiancée yet. Not that it's any business of yours.'

Gracie remembered what he'd said before she'd opened her big mouth and said rebelliously, 'If I did serve up fish fingers you'd have no one to blame but yourself.'

Once again she had the curious feeling that he was holding back a laugh, but then he glowered at her. 'Don't even think about it.'

'Was that all?'

He nodded curtly, and before Gracie did or said something she'd really regret she turned and fled.

Rocco watched Gracie's slim back retreating through his offices. He didn't miss the fact that she caught the eye of more than one male employee, or that it made his insides tighten. How did she have the singular ability to constantly make him veer off course and gravitate towards her?

Her observation about his offices being too transparent had never been made before—by anyone. He felt inordinately exposed, because only he knew that his preoccupation with being able to see all around him came from his early days and the constant need to watch his back. It was also why he surrounded himself with people when he knew most others in his position preferred solitude. On some level, because he'd grown up surrounded by so many, it was one thing he hadn't been able to let go of, and she'd effortlessly spotted it. Albeit without understanding it.

Most people assumed it was an aesthetic thing. But it was as if she'd *known* there was more to it. And then that comment about always striving to be at the highest point. Literally.

She disappeared into the elevator and Rocco sat down and swung his chair around to the view, so no one could see him. For the first time he actually did resent the lack of privacy. He rested his elbows on the armrests of his chair and his chin on steepled fingers. In that moment a very illicit and long-buried feeling of rebellion stirred his blood.

Mid-afternoon that day, Gracie was neck-deep in preparing her menu for the evening. She was hot and sweaty when George appeared in the kitchen, holding out a big white box.

'For you, from the boss.'

Gracie wiped her hands on her apron and took it. Her silly heart started to thump. Some rogue part of her brain seemed to run away with itself and she couldn't help imagining a beautiful chiffon dress in delicate shades of pink. And for a moment she couldn't help fantasising that dinner this evening was for *her* and Rocco.

She laid the box on the table and opened it up with unsteady hands. It only took a few seconds for those traitorous images to crumble to dust. She reached in and pulled out a black pinafore dress and a white apron. Sheer tights and plain black court shoes. A note fell out too. The arrogant scrawl said, *'Please wear this later. R.'*

Gracie alternately felt like laughing and crying. She'd never before allowed herself to daydream such fantasies even for a moment. Her life had been about gritty reality from day one. She'd had one boyfriend and he'd never given her anything—not even a birthday card. And suddenly she was indulging in Cinderella-esque dreams?

Disgusted with herself, Gracie stuffed the dress back into the box, childishly hoping it would get creased. She returned to her preparations and took a deep breath, curbing the desire to walk down to Rocco's gleaming office and tip the sauce she'd been preparing over his smarmy head.

CHAPTER FIVE

PACING in his drawing room that evening, Rocco couldn't remember the last time he'd been so tense. He'd come back to the apartment about thirty minutes before and had headed for the kitchen—only to find the door locked. He'd knocked on the door, to hear Gracie call from inside, 'Go away. I'm busy.'

He'd called through the door, 'I hope you have everything in hand.'

'Oh, don't worry,' she'd sung out sweetly. 'I do. The fish fingers are almost done.'

Rocco had bitten back the urge to demand she open up immediately. He'd never been kept so consistently in an uncomfortable state of arousal in his life, and it had nothing to do with the woman due to walk in the door at any moment and everything to do with the woman a few feet away, behind the closed kitchen door. The woman related to the man who had set out to destroy his reputation and steal from him. The woman to whom he'd all but handed a sterling opportunity to humiliate him this evening.

A discreet knock on the door at that moment heralded his security man showing Honora Winthrop into the drawing room. The door opened to reveal the icy beauty looking predictably stunning in a black silk draped dress which managed the amazing feat of being completely modest while at the same time daringly see-through.

The immediately negative effect on Rocco's libido was almost comical. She was effectively better than a cold shower. But, with smooth smile in place, Rocco went forward to greet her, pushing aside all visions of a red-haired temptress.

Gracie heard the voices outside in the drawing room and took a deep shaky breath. Much to her chagrin, the dress Rocco had sent was not creased. It was also about a size too small, proving to be a very snug fit around her breasts, bottom and thighs. At first she'd cursed him for doing it on purpose, but then had had to figure that it was far more likely to be because he had no interest in her body, therefore why would be have any notion, or care, what size she was?

She smoothed the small frilled white apron and tried once again to pull the dress down a little further to her knee. She tidied her hair, which she'd pulled back into a high bun, and picked up the tray that held two ice-misted glasses of champagne and a couple of small plates with crushed olive *vol-au-vents* and crab canapés.

When she walked into the room the voices died away. Gracie was burningly aware of two sets of eyes, one of which was dark and lingered, the other which glanced away again almost immediately. *It must be the woman from the paper.* Gracie was peripherally aware of a statuesque blonde beauty standing near Rocco at the window.

He surprised her by coming forward and taking the tray out of her hands. 'Thank you, Gracie. We'll eat in twenty minutes.'

She released the tray and tried to read the ambiguous look in his eyes, but couldn't. So she turned and forced herself to walk away, when all she wanted to do was run. Back in the kitchen she laid her face against the door for a moment. She was shaking. Thankfully Rocco hadn't expected her to hand out the drinks and canapés. She would have expected that he'd make the most of a moment like that and it was disconcerting that he hadn't.

Pushing herself off the door, she went to finalise preparations for the starter and forced from her head images of Rocco and that woman toasting each other with the sparkling drink.

Rocco couldn't get the image of Gracie walking into the drawing room out of his head. He felt as if it would be seared there for ever. Clearly the uniform he'd organised had come in a size too small. It was plastered to her petite lithe body, showing off the curves that were normally hidden. A button strained across her chest. The dress's hem rested teasingly above her knee, revealing pale and slender legs. It was more like a French maid's outfit for a hen night than the sophisticated serving dress he'd expected. And he had no one to blame but himself.

'Rocco?'

Rocco broke out of his trance and looked at the woman beside him, one finely drawn eyebrow arched above perfectly made-up blue eyes.

He smiled tightly. 'Forgive me…'

Gracie had just served the starter, and put her ear to the door to try and hear the conversation, or any observation about the food. She heard Rocco's low voice, and then an irritating tinkling laugh followed by, *'Oh, Rocco, you're terrible!'*

Gracie's face burned. She felt paranoid, as if Rocco might come back through the door and hold up his plate with its linguine and truffle starter and say, *Seriously? You thought this would be suitable?*

But he didn't appear. So Gracie got on with the main course.

After a suitable amount of time she went in to check the wine levels and saw that Rocco had finished his starter but Ms Winthrop's was half eaten. The woman barely glanced at Gracie, just pushed her plate slightly towards the edge of the table, clearly indicating that she was finished.

Gracie curbed her tongue when she got a warning glance from Rocco, and replenished the wine and took the plates away, also curbing a cheeky urge to curtsey.

When she brought in the main course Gracie couldn't help the dart of satisfaction at seeing Rocco's eyes widen. The smell of the guinea fowl *cacciatore* was impressively aromatic. She deftly served them both, and left again. She was starting to get seriously annoyed with Rocco's date's complete lack of acknowledgment. At least in the bar where she'd worked—as rough as it had been—people looked you in the eye and not through you.

She started clearing up, valiantly ignoring the hum of voices and trying not to imagine what they might be talking about. Wedding plans? Gracie slapped down the tea-towel at the spiking of irrational jealousy.

Any kind of feelings for Rocco de Marco beyond antipathy and extreme wariness were so patently futile that—

Gracie heard a noise and whirled around to see George coming in through the other kitchen door, which opened out to the entrance hall. She'd given him an early supper of the same food she was serving Rocco and his guest because he'd finished his shift.

He had a big grin on his face and patted his enormous belly. 'That was the singularly most amazing meal I've ever eaten.'

Gracie grinned. 'Really? Oh, George, thank you!' And she jumped up to give him a quick impetuous kiss, as much for his human affection and their growing friendship as anything else. Just then the other door opened and Gracie sprang back, cheeks burning.

Rocco stood there, looking like thunder, with his napkin in his hand. 'If you're quite ready? We've finished in here.'

George scuttled out as fast as he could for such a huge man, and Gracie leapt to attention, feeling absurdly guilty for no reason. Rocco stayed at the door, forcing her to go past him, and when her hip came into contact with his body she had to stop herself from flinching away. Even that small contact with his tall, hard-muscled body was seismic to her system. She cleared away the plates, glad for the first time that evening that the cold-looking blonde beauty wasn't looking at her.

When she'd composed herself as much as she could, she went back in with the lemon torte dessert and coffee. Ms Winthrop was saying, 'Darling, how on earth did you entice Louis away from the Four Seasons? Roberto must be simply livid! That meal was divine.'

A dart of satisfaction went through Gracie as she put down the tray on the nearby serving table. In the silence that followed she found she was holding her breath, waiting to see what Rocco would say. As the seconds ticked past it became incredibly important.

She was picking up the dessert plates and feeling sick inside when he cleared his throat. 'Actually, Louis was indisposed this evening. So Gracie here, who is my temporary housekeeper, prepared our meal.'

Gracie walked over and put down the plates. She felt a little light-headed for a moment. She couldn't believe Rocco had actually credited her. For the first time all evening the blonde shot her a narrow-eyed and very assessing glance.

'Oh…how quaint.'

The words dripped with condescension.

That glance had obviously taken in a multitude of facts, because she looked back to Rocco and said, very deliberately, 'I wasn't going to say anything, but I thought perhaps Louis was on an off-night or had sent one of his sous-chefs. The guinea fowl *did* taste slightly odd. I do hope she knew what she was doing, I have an important family function tomorrow. I can't afford to be ill.'

Gracie was rooted to the spot for a long moment. She couldn't believe that this woman was picking apart her efforts as if she wasn't even there. She registered a quick glance from Rocco, but was too stunned to look at him. She whirled around and escaped back to the kitchen, hearing his low tones as she went, but unable to make out the words.

Gracie was shaking—first of all with shock that Rocco had spoken up for her. She'd fully expected him to humiliate her by denying her contribution, but he'd sounded almost *proud*. And then shock morphed to anger at that woman's downright rudeness.

She heard a laugh coming from the drawing room—*her* irritating laugh. To Gracie's abject horror emotion surged, making hot tears prick at the back of her eyes as she looked at the chaos spread around the kitchen, the fruits of her hard labours.

She wasn't sure what had happened, but at some point she'd started cooking for *Rocco*. George had told her where he was from in Italy, and that had informed her choices. Even whilst hating herself for her weakness, she'd wanted to impress him. Perhaps she'd hoped he would see that she wasn't just some nobody who had nothing to offer except for a tenuous link to her brother?

She heard a door slam and flinched. No doubt that was Rocco and his date leaving for an exclusive club in town. Gracie wiped at her cheeks and set about cleaning up through a blur of tears.

She didn't hear the door open, so when she heard a soft, 'Gracie,' from behind her she dropped a pan on the marble floor.

Gracie whirled around, too startled to remember how she must look. Her eyes cleared but her cheeks still stung. Rocco was standing there, his jacket removed and his tie undone and loose as if he'd yanked at it impatiently. The top button of his shirt was open and his hair was dishevelled.

Gracie took all this in in a split second. 'I heard the front door,' she said dumbly, wondering if he was some kind of mirage. 'I thought you'd left.'

Rocco shook his head. His hands were deep in his pockets and even now Gracie had to fight the impulse to let her gaze drop.

His voice was tight. 'Miss Winthrop has gone home, and she won't be back. I must apologise for her rudeness. She refused to come in here and do it herself.'

Gracie's mouth opened and closed like a fish. 'You asked her to come in here? And apologise?'

Rocco nodded curtly. 'I shouldn't have even had to ask. She had no right to talk to you like that. And she was wrong. You served up an amazing meal.' He shook his head slightly. 'I had no idea you could cook like that.'

Half dazed, Gracie said, 'One of my foster parents trained in Paris as a chef in the sixties. She ended up working as a cook in a school kitchen when she came back to England because no one would hire a female chef.' Gracie shrugged. 'I'm not that proficient, really... I picked up some basics and I like cooking.'

Rocco stepped further into the kitchen and Gracie gulped. He looked so *intent*. She moved back a step and her foot knocked the pan on the floor. She looked down to see that some sauce had leaked out and automatically bent down to get it. Suddenly Rocco was there, taking her arm and helping her up, taking the pan out of her hand.

He led her away from the spill. 'No,' he said, his accent thick. 'Someone else will clean it up.'

Gracie just looked up at him. He was too close all of a sudden, his sheer physical presence more than overwhelming, and she was horribly aware of her red eyes. She hated that she had been so upset and was terrified Rocco would see it.

'You don't have to apologise. She's the one who was rude.'

'But I put you in that position. I let her speak to you like that.'

Gracie couldn't keep the hurt from her voice. 'Yes,' she said, 'you did. I thought you did it on purpose. To get some pleasure out of seeing me squirm. Seeing me out of my depth.'

Rocco shook his head, and the look on his face made tendrils of heat coil up inside her—along with panic. She didn't know if she could control her response when Rocco stood this close to her, touching her. And that awful uncontrollable emotion was rising again, that sense of how vulnerable she'd felt this evening. She hadn't felt a need to impress someone for a long time—if ever.

Gracie spoke with a rush. 'She looked through me, and then she looked at me as if I was dirt, as if she couldn't believe that I'd actually handled her food.'

'I'm sorry,' he said.

Confusion warred alongside the panic within Gracie. She didn't know what Rocco was trying to do to her. He was looking at her so intensely. 'Stop saying that. You're not sorry at all.'

Tears were blurring her vision again, and Gracie fought not to let them fall, blinking rapidly. He'd reduced her to a snivelling wreck—why wasn't he walking away? Anger at her response, and at him for precipitating it, made her lash out as she tried to extricate her arm from his grip.

'Do you know what it's like to be looked through? As if you don't exist? Do you have any idea how that feels? I am *someone*, Rocco. I am a person with hopes and dreams and feelings. I'm not a bad person, despite what you might think. When someone looks through you like you're invisible—'

'Gracie…'

Rocco had taken both her arms in his hands now. He was standing right in front of her, gripping her tight. She sucked in a shaky breath.

He spoke again. 'I know…I know what it's like.'

Faint scorn laced Gracie's voice. 'How can *you* know? You have no idea what I'm talking about.'

His hands gripped tighter. There was a white line of tension around his mouth and his eyes were blazing. 'I *know*.'

His hands gentled then, and Gracie stared up, dumbfounded. One hand came up to her chin and with his thumb and forefinger he tipped her face up higher, so she couldn't escape his gaze.

'I see you.'

Emotions were roiling in Gracie's belly. She felt hot all over. Confusion warred with the anger inside her, and she shook her head. 'You don't… You can't. I'm nothing to you.'

Fiercely, he shook his head. 'No. You are *not* nothing.'

Gracie was dimly aware that in their backward-forward dance they had now moved into a more dimly lit corner of the kitchen by the window seat. She could feel her hair unravelling. The entire world might have stopped turning in that moment and she wouldn't have noticed. All she could see were the black depths of Rocco's eyes and she was drowning. She had to fight the pull of the strongest tide she'd ever felt.

'Rocco…' Her voice was shaky. 'What are you doing? Why are you here?'

Her lower arms were between them, as if she was still valiantly making the effort to pull free from Rocco's hands. But his hands had gentled, and yet Gracie couldn't move back or break free. Some fatal lethargy had invaded her bones and her blood. He pulled her in closer.

He didn't speak for a long moment, and then it was as if the words were being pulled out from deep inside him. 'I want you. I am here because I want *you*. This whole evening, this past week, ever since I met you…I've wanted you. Not her. She guessed how I felt. That's why she was so cruel.'

Gracie shook her head even as molten heat seemed to bloom down low between her legs. She'd never felt so *hot*. And so out of her depth. She'd truly believed that her guilty little secret of obsessing about Rocco would never be noticed. Or reciprocated.

Gracie shook her head again, more forcefully this time. 'No. You're bored…or trying to make her jealous or something. I'm just convenient.'

Rocco grimaced then. 'You're definitely not convenient. And I am not bored. I don't care if she *is* jealous, because it's over and I'm never going to see her again.'

Gracie reeled. The full magnitude of what he was saying started to sink in. He'd had a fight with his fiancée over *her*? And he'd chosen *her*?

'But…you had a relationship. You were going to marry her.'

Rocco went still for a second as the enormity of her words sank in. He had just ended his relationship with Honora Winthrop, and in doing so his grand plans to marry her. He'd done it because he wanted to sleep with Gracie O'Brien more urgently than he'd ever wanted anything in his life. More than the social acceptance he'd hungered for for so long? He didn't even want to answer that.

In some rational part of his brain that was still functioning Rocco knew very well that if he ran after Honora Winthrop and caught her just as she reached home he might salvage something.

And like a slow-dawning yet cataclysmic realisation he knew he didn't want to. The feeling of claustrophobia that had been dogging him for weeks had lifted.

Rocco shook his head. 'We didn't have a relationship— not really. What we had was an understanding that a more permanent relationship would be mutually beneficial on many levels.'

'But that's…so cold.'

Rocco shrugged and said cynically, 'That's life. I hadn't yet asked her to marry me, and I haven't been sleeping with her.'

Gracie was trying to take it all in. She knew that Rocco wouldn't feel he had to hand her platitudes to get her into bed. She believed that he hadn't cared for that woman, and that he hadn't slept with her. He was too powerful to care about lying. She knew he wouldn't shy away from hurting her with the truth if he *had* slept with that woman.

Her head started to throb. She couldn't take any more in. She didn't want to hear anything else. Rocco pulled her even closer. She felt as if she was on a train with only one destination and there was no way she could get off now. Unconsciously she'd gone up on tiptoe, her body knowing what it wanted even before she did.

His head lowered towards hers, that beautiful mouth came closer and closer, and Gracie's eyelids fluttered closed just as darkness and heat swept over her mouth and settled there like a brand.

At first the kiss was like falling into a whirlpool. Instinctively Gracie reached out to hold onto Rocco's shirt because she couldn't feel her legs any more. And then an urgency gripped them both, as if the first taste was merely a civilised veneer. Rocco's hands went to Gracie's face. She was being backed against a wall, or some sort of solid surface, and Gracie leaned back and let it support her weight.

Rocco's mouth was hard, and yet his lips were soft, pressing, tasting, coaxing. She felt the slide of his tongue against the closed seam of her lips and her hands clenched tighter as her mouth opened up to Rocco. The kiss deepened. His chest pressed hard against her, crushing her hands between them. But Gracie didn't care. She revelled in Rocco's big hands holding her face just so he could plunder her mouth.

Gracie was falling, slipping and sliding into another dimension. Rocco's scent intoxicated her. His tongue stroked along hers in a wicked caress. Teeth nipped at her lower lip, only to soothe it in the same moment. It was tart and sweet all at once. It was all-consuming, like jumping right into the middle of a fire.

He took his mouth away and amidst the fiery excitement pressed a kiss to the corner of her mouth—an incongruously gentle gesture. Gracie opened heavy eyelids. Her mouth felt bruised, swollen. She wouldn't be surprised if the world had moved on a couple of decades since they'd started kissing. She felt that altered.

She looked straight up into the dark molten pools of Rocco's eyes. This close she could see flecks of gold. His cheeks were flushed.

Feeling bewildered, she asked shakily, 'What is this?'

Rocco took down his hands from her face and caught some of her hair, wrapping it around a finger, looking at the fiery gold strands.

'This…' his gaze came back up '…is called chemistry—except I've never felt it like this before.'

Gracie shook her head. 'I've never felt this before either.'

Rocco's hand moved slowly up over Gracie's hip to her waist, and then under one arm to rest where her breast curved out. With a lazy smile Rocco moved his hand so it cupped her breast, the thumb moving back and forth over the taut peak which tightened even more underneath the stiff material of her dress. Her breath hitched.

'This,' Rocco continued, 'is what started between us the night we met.'

Gracie's eyes searched Rocco's for sincerity. So he'd felt it too. This extraordinary connection. Like a livewire coming to life the moment she'd looked at him. This had nothing to do with her brother. This had existed between them before they'd even known who the other was.

Suddenly a desperate urgency Gracie had never felt before rushed through her body. She needed to connect on a base level with this man right now. She lifted her hands from between them and caught his head, his hair soft and silky between her fingers. Inexorably she brought his head down to hers and pressed her mouth to his. He took her cue and both hands moved to grip her waist tightly as his mouth opened and his natural dominance took over.

Tongues met and clashed furiously. Gracie arched herself into the hard wall of his chest, crushing her breasts to him, desperately seeking to assuage the ache building throughout her whole body and between her legs. Their hips were tight together. Gracie could feel the long ridge of his arousal and instinctively opened her legs to increase the contact and friction.

She was barely aware of Rocco tugging the tiny apron free and moving his hands to the buttons of her dress, ripping them apart. Cool air touched her heated skin and she craved to be free of her constricting garments, nearly sobbing out loud when she felt Rocco's big hands pull the top of the dress apart to bare her breasts to his gaze. She vaguely heard material rip.

He drew back from the kiss and looked down, breathing harshly. Gracie was dizzy, heart racing like an express train. She couldn't get enough oxygen to her brain. Rocco's eyes were feverish. As much as he could he pushed the shoulders of her dress down, baring even more of her breasts. The pale skin was framed by a black bra, not racy in the slightest. But Gracie was beyond caring. She needed this man's touch, his mouth…

As if reading her mind, Rocco pulled down one cup, forcing her plump breast to spring free. As if hypnotised, Rocco cupped and caressed her breast, a thumb stroking the peak back and forth. Gracie bit her lip to stop herself from begging.

Excitement zinged through her veins when his dark head lowered and finally the wet sucking heat of his mouth surrounded that taut peak. His tongue rolled around it, sucking it into even more tightness. Gracie's head fell back against the wall, the pain unnoticed in the haze of pleasure infusing her body. Her hips were squirming, undulating against Rocco's, her legs had parted even more and his erection was long and hard and thick against her sensitive sex.

Gracie wanted to see him unclothed and started searching for his shirt, clumsy hands fumbling with his buttons. He took his mouth away from her breast and stood up.

Rocco's head was consumed by fire. A fire of lust and desire and need too great to deny. Gracie was half slumped against the wall behind her. His hips grinding into hers was probably the only thing still keeping her standing. Her mouth was dark pink and swollen. Eyes huge with pupils so dilated they looked black.

Her fast breaths made her pale breasts rise and fall enticingly. She had small tight pink nipples, surrounded by slightly darker areolae and freckles. Rocco felt a sense of inevitability sink into his bones. This woman was *his*.

He knew he couldn't rationalise that assertion now. He could only act on the singularly strongest driving force of his life: to have her and make her his.

With impatience making his usually graceful movements jerky, Rocco opened his shirt, buttons popping off around them. He looked at Gracie's half-open dress. It had to come off over her head. He brought his hands to the thin material and ripped it all the way to the hem. His blood was pumping now. Her dress gaped open down to her thighs, giving a glimpse of black panties.

He felt feral. He felt wild. He'd never felt like this with another woman.

He looked at Gracie and forced himself to grind out, 'We're doing this right here, right now. Unless you say no. You have about ten seconds to decide.'

CHAPTER SIX

GRACIE looked up at Rocco, towering above her, making her feel impossibly small and delicate. The sheer stark hunger stamped onto his features was awesome and almost frightening. But she wasn't frightened. She hadn't even blinked when he'd ripped her dress open like some kind of animal. It had excited her.

She shook her head and reached out a hand to his belt. 'Don't stop.'

He seemed to wait for an infinitesimal moment, as if testing her resolve, and then with a guttural sound he took off his shirt and started to push Gracie's dress down her arms until it was off completely. Her bra came off too, so now she was naked except for her knickers. She felt vulnerable for a moment, until Rocco started undoing his belt and trousers. And then heat took over again.

She greedily took in his amazing physique. Taut muscles and gleaming skin. Springy dark hair on his chest that arrowed down into that tantalising line which was revealed as his trousers slid down over powerful thighs. He wore snug fitting briefs that were tented over his erection. Gracie's eyes went wide.

But then Rocco reached for her and she looked up, her gaze clashing with his. It was as if they were in the eye of the storm. Suddenly everything took on a languorous feel. His hands tangled in her hair, tumbling it from its bun completely. His mouth found hers, kissing her, rediscovering her taste with his tongue. And then it moved down, over her shoulder and to her breasts, which felt full and aching. Both hands cupped her breasts and he fed one hard peak and then the other into his mouth, teeth nipping gently, making Gracie cry out.

The urgency didn't take long to build again. Gracie was straining against Rocco, her back arched, hips moving impatiently. One of his hands moved around her rib cage and down her back, under her knickers to cup the cheek of her bottom, squeezing it harshly, making her nerve-points tighten and tingle.

His mouth moved back up to find hers, and he pulled her close making his chest hairs scrape against moist, sensitised nipples. Gracie was clutching at his shoulders, incapable of doing anything but succumbing to this onslaught on her senses. His hand moved from her bottom, tugging her panties down slightly, and around to the apex of her legs, between their bodies.

Gracie held her breath as his long fingers explored the damp curls surrounding her sex. Her hands gripped his wide shoulders as a finger delved deeper into the secret folds where she ached. He found the most intimate part of her and rubbed back and forth. Gracie started to shake.

Rocco's finger thrust deep inside, the invasion all at once shocking and cataclysmic. Gracie came in a rush, her body convulsing around Rocco's hand. The sudden tide of pleasure was so intense that tears leaked from her eyes, her whole body held taut for a long moment.

When it was over Rocco slowly withdrew his hand. Gracie felt shell-shocked, numb, with little fires of sensation racing over her skin. She'd never experienced anything like that. All she could remember of her few sexual experiences was how she'd never found any kind of satisfaction. She'd thought sex was overrated. She couldn't believe she'd just—

Suddenly she was being lifted. Rocco said roughly, 'Put your legs around my waist.'

Dumbly, she did so, wrapping them around him, feet locked together over his buttocks, arms around his neck. He walked them over to the huge table where they usually ate breakfast. Holding her securely with one strong arm, he used his other one to sweep the detritus on the table to the floor. Cookery books landed with dull thuds and a cup fell and smashed. Rocco laid her on her back, the apex of her thighs tight against his waist. She could feel his erection nudging her bottom and her sated body started to hum again.

Rocco gently disengaged her legs, all the time staring down at her if mesmerised by her. He hooked his hands into his briefs and with a quick downward movement tugged them off. Gracie looked down to see the full extent of his erection. It had felt big. But it looked massive. Shivers of fear at his size mixed with excitement went through her like electric rivers of shock.

His hands were on her panties, tugging them down. Gracie lifted her hips silently. Their eyes met. She saw Rocco's gaze go to the golden-red curls between her legs. His chest expanded and his eyes grew even darker. And then he was pushing her legs apart with those big hands and his head was going down...

Her heart stopped. He wasn't—no one had ever before—

And then she felt his breath cool against her hot skin, and her hands clenched into fists when she felt the first sweep of his tongue down her moist cleft. A shudder of pure ecstasy went through her as his tongue dipped and swirled and teased her. She could feel herself tensing again, the imminent onset of pleasure very obvious, and suddenly she couldn't bear for him to see how easily he could make her orgasm and lose control as she already had.

She tried to bring her thighs together, hands searching for his head, pulling on his hair before it was too late. She could already feel her muscles clenching and unclenching in preparation.

'No…*stop*…it's too much.'

Rocco finally seemed to hear her and came up over her like some kind of avenging dark angel. His body was tall and lean, and so powerful he took her breath away, making her forget everything else.

She was vaguely aware of him donning a protective sheath, and then with his hand between them and an intense look on his face she could feel the wide blunt head of him seek entrance at her moist core.

The intrusion made her suck her breath in. She looked down at their bodies to see the pale skin of her thighs tight against his hips. He was slowly and inexorably sinking into her, pushing and stretching her body. The full feeling was almost excruciating, and she put a hand out as if to stop him, but it came into contact with his tight abdomen muscles, damp with sweat, and fresh heat flooded her, easing his passage into her body.

After an infinitesimal moment, he was in all the way. She could feel his body snug against hers. She felt impossibly impaled, but even as she thought that awareness sank in and tiny tremors of pleasure pulsed through her. Almost slowly, Rocco started to move out again, and those pleasurable tremors increased, making Gracie arch her back towards him.

He bent his head and took one rosy nipple into his mouth, suckling fiercely as he began the inexorable ride back into her body. This time the ease of movement was markedly different. Gracie's muscles clenched around him, as if loath to let him go.

Any hint of restraint was a thin veneer, hiding their increasing urgency. Gracie locked her legs around Rocco's hips, forcing him even closer. His strokes became more urgent, harder and deeper. Gracie could feel the rush of pleasure coming towards her. As she began to lose herself in the flooding warmth of her second orgasm in the space of minutes she could see the intensity of Rocco's expression. He was holding back until she came. An extraordinary tenderness overwhelmed her just as the most powerful euphoric bliss broke her in two. What she'd felt before had been a mere precursor to this ecstasy.

Rocco pounded into her body. Her muscles clenched around his thick shaft as he too finally gave in and allowed his body to succumb to his own climax.

Finally a brief calm seemed to descend, and the only sound that could be heard was their ragged breathing. Gracie became aware of her legs locked around Rocco's waist, his damp chest crushing her pleasurably to the cool hard surface of the table.

Registering that was like a cold douche of water.

She tensed all over. She was naked, on her back with her legs clamped around Rocco's hips, in the harsh glow of the kitchen lights. And Rocco de Marco was between her legs, her body still holding his in an intimate embrace.

Before that reality could intrude too much Rocco raised himself off her and looked down, his hair flopping sexily over his forehead. Gracie could feel him inside her, and unbelievably he was still slightly hard.

As if reading the direction of her thoughts he smiled tightly. 'If we don't move, I think there's going to be a repeat performance very soon.'

He drew back and disengaged from her body. Immediately Gracie felt bereft and very naked. Until Rocco scooped her up into his arms and walked out of the kitchen, carefully avoiding the destruction they'd left on the floor, and through the silent apartment to his bedroom. He deposited her on the bed as gently as if she were made of china and went into the bathroom. She heard the sound of a shower running.

Rocco came back out and scooped her up again, as if she weighed no more than a bag of sugar, and within seconds she was gasping on wobbly legs under a powerfully warm spray. Rocco was soaping his hands and running them all over her body, washing her, and Gracie gave up trying to rationalise this and stood silently while Rocco thoroughly soaped her whole body.

When his hand slipped between her legs she widened slumberous eyes and her breath hitched. He was so virile and gorgeous, hair plastered to his skull, water running in rivulets down his face and over hard chest muscles. And those wicked long fingers were stroking between her legs, making her moan softly.

With a rueful smile Rocco took his hand away and shook his head. 'I think you need a break before we indulge again.'

Again. Gracie grew hot just thinking of all that passionate intensity *again*. She didn't know if she could cope.

Rocco was pouring shampoo into his hand and turning her around so that he could wash her hair. She was glad not to be the focus of that black gaze for a moment.

After a few seconds she heard him say behind her, 'You weren't a virgin?'

Gracie grew tense. She shook her head and said huskily, 'No. I've had sex before…'

Familiar pain gripped her when she thought of the boy

she'd trusted enough to sleep with her at her last foster home. She'd been just eighteen, so young and vulnerable. Steven had been in jail and she'd been desperately lonely. But as soon as he'd slept with her he'd dumped her, telling her that no one wanted to go out with a slag.

He'd spread the word among their peers and Gracie had been branded an easy lay, which had been so far from the truth that she hadn't trusted anyone since then. She'd escaped to college soon after, and had kept herself to herself.

Yet within days of meeting Rocco de Marco she was allowing him to seduce her on a kitchen table as if she'd done it all her life.

'But it's been a while?'

His voice cut off her tumultuous thoughts. Gracie was mortified. Had it been that obvious? She nodded her head quickly. Rocco stepped up close behind her then, and she went properly weak at the knees feeling that powerfully muscular body along the length of hers, his recovered erection between them. She fought not to move her hips against him as wantonly as she wanted to, awfully conscious of her vulnerability.

His arms came under her arms and his hands cupped her soapy breasts, trapping her nipples. His head came down and he said softly, 'You were so tight around me. I liked it.'

Gracie's feeling of vulnerability dissolved when she remembered how he'd felt when he'd thrust into her that first moment. She turned in his arms and looked up shyly. 'I liked it too…'

He just looked at her for a long moment, while the water beat down around them, and then he moved her so that she stood under the spray, to rinse all the shampoo and soap from her hair and body. His touch was no longer seductive, it was brisk.

Then he flipped off the shower and grabbed two towels, enveloping her in one. He handed her out of the shower first, and then stepped out too. It was as if a cold wind had sprung up between them and Gracie felt on edge. Had she said something wrong? Been too easy? How could she explain to him that it felt as if on some level she'd known him for ever—as if her body knew exactly how to be with him? How to pleasure him? That she wasn't like this normally?

She'd had no idea desire could consume her like a forest fire raging through dry wood. She watched as he turned away from her to rub himself dry roughly. Even now her eyes couldn't help devouring him, lingering on the way his muscles bunched and stretched.

Hesitantly she forced herself to ask, 'Are you...is everything okay?'

His hands stopped in their movement. And then he said gruffly, without looking at her, 'Why wouldn't it be?'

He sounded so remote and harsh that Gracie took a step back, clutching the towel to her. 'If you regret what just happened—'

He whirled around fast and snaked the towel around his hips. He glared at her. 'Why on earth would I regret it? It's the best sex I've ever had.'

Gracie blanched and then felt hot. His use of the word *sex* scored at her insides like a knife. 'Well, you don't have to sound so angry about it. It doesn't have to happen again.'

If anything that made him look even fiercer. He stepped close to her, jaw tight. 'That was not a one-off. It will be happening again, and it'll keep happening until we burn ourselves free of this insanity.'

Familiar fire rose within Gracie at his temper and his autocratic tone. She straightened her shoulders. 'Well, for your information, I think I've had enough. I don't need to burn myself free of *anything*. This was a really bad idea.'

Gracie grabbed the towel around her and went to step around Rocco to leave the bathroom, but he halted her progress with his hands on her shoulders. She glared at him as fiercely as he was glaring at her. The air crackled around them.

'Where do you think you're going?'

Gracie tossed her head, 'Oh, so now I'm a prisoner of this room? Not just your apartment?'

'Damn it, woman,' Rocco growled, and hauled her close. Before she knew what was happening he was kissing her, forcing her head back, mouth crushing hers. Defiant to the end she kept her mouth closed and stayed stiff. Until she started to feel dizzy and had to breathe in.

Rocco seized his moment and his tongue invaded her mouth with shockingly hot intimacy. He pulled her hips into his at the same time and she could feel the resurgence of his desire. Suddenly she was back in that mad vortex, with need clawing through her worse than before. Because now she'd tasted Rocco, felt the full force of him…and of course she couldn't turn her back on this any more than he could. Her bones turned to liquid and her tongue duelled with his, their mouths tight together as if in danger of being ripped apart at any moment.

He tore his mouth away after long, dizzying seconds and said gutturally, 'I won't take you like an animal again.'

He bent down and lifted her into his arms, strode back into the bedroom. He put her down on the bed and stripped the towel from around his waist. Gracie's eyes were glued to him as he came down over her, twitching her towel aside so he could feast his eyes on her body, laid out for him. He reminded her of some mythical pagan god. She'd sensed a raw wildness in him the night she'd met him, but the reality of it was intoxicating.

He trailed the back of his hand from the valley of her

breasts to the juncture of her thighs. She squirmed and bit her lip even as she wanted to have the strength to grab his hand and throw it aside, to tell him that she wouldn't succumb to him again.

He pushed her thighs apart with one hand and pressed his palm against her. He looked deep into her eyes, 'You're mine, Gracie O'Brien, and I'm going to make you mine over and over again—until you don't even know who you are any more.'

'I'm going to make you mine over and over again—until you don't even know who you are any more.'

Rocco was standing at the window of his bedroom with his back to the view of a faint pink dawn breaking over London's skyline. His arms were crossed and he was looking warily at the woman sleeping in his bed, as if she might jump out at any moment and grab him. He felt as if he'd just been catapulted back into reality after a psychedelic mind-altering experience.

Those words were reverberating in his head. When he'd said them to her he'd meant that he wanted to make her forget her own name because she'd made him forget...*everything*. Who he was. What he was. *Why* he was.

It had only been in the shower, as she'd looked up at him with those dark serious eyes, that the first sliver of sanity had returned—and with it the awful, excoriating realisation that he'd exposed himself comprehensively.

Acute vulnerability of a kind he hadn't felt in years— so long ago that he'd hardly recognised it—had burnt him up inside and he'd lashed out. But Gracie had stood up to him, like she had from day one, and he'd soon been fired up all over again, that feeling of vulnerability dissolving like a mist to be replaced with sheer lust.

Last night had proved to him that for all his hard-won

control and precious rationale he couldn't keep from acting on base desire. Once he'd touched Gracie there had been no going back. He grimaced. There had been no going back from the moment he'd seen her standing in that elevator, looking so pale and anxious.

And from the moment she'd walked into the drawing room in that provocative uniform Rocco had bitterly regretted that Honora Winthrop was there. If he'd ever needed a stark comparison between two women they'd unwittingly provided it. As the evening had unfolded, and Gracie had served them exquisite dish after exquisite dish, Rocco had become more and more entranced. More and more surprised that she wasn't using the opportunity to humiliate him. And more and more certain that he wanted her.

He'd battled an increasing need to *see* her. He'd suffered through the courses, tuning out Honora Winthrop's cut-glass tones, and come to life each time Gracie came back into the room, eyes devouring her, painfully aware of his state of arousal—for *her*.

He'd become so impatient at one stage that he'd gone looking for her himself, only to see her stretching up to kiss his own security man sweetly on the cheek. He'd looked as if he'd just received a bonus. The jealousy had been swift and shocking. He'd wanted to fire George on the spot and shake Gracie until she rattled.

When Honora had made those snide comments about the food Rocco had had to restrain himself from reaching across the table and pushing her sanctimoniously perfect face into her dessert. As soon as Gracie had walked out of the room he'd stood up and told Honora coolly, 'This evening is over. Thank you for coming, but I think we both know that this won't go any further.'

She had stood up too, quiveringly angry. She'd spat at

him, 'It's over because you want that tart of a housekeeper?
Is *that* why you've refused to sleep with me?' Before he
could answer she'd said, 'You don't get it, do you? You can
have me and still have *her*. That's how it's done. I would
only expect discretion. You can sleep with who you want
while we maintain the façade of a happy marriage.'

She had articulated exactly what he'd set out to achieve
by wooing her into marriage, and suddenly Rocco had re-
coiled from her words as if they were poisonous. Tight-
lipped, he'd said, 'Get out. I've changed my mind.'

Honora had just shaken her head, eyes as cold as ice
and full of malicious pity. 'You won't get another chance
like this.'

He'd all but snarled at her, 'I'll make my chances—just
as I've always done. Now, what I'd like you to do first is
apologise to Gracie for your rudeness and then leave.'

She'd thrown her head back and laughed. And then she'd
walked out, slamming the door behind her.

Now, in the early-morning light, Rocco could hardly
believe that he'd so spectacularly ruined his reputation in
one fell swoop. He knew someone like Honora Winthrop
would waste no time in spreading the word, along with half
a dozen untruths, so that her own reputation wasn't dam-
aged. He wouldn't get so close to a society darling again
for a long time. They were a closely knit clique. And yet he
couldn't seem to drum up any urgency to want to rectify
the situation. Not when he was looking at the woman on
the bed, sprawled in voluptuous abandon, with the marks
of their passionate lovemaking on her delicately pale skin.

Wild red curls and waves rippled around her head across
the stark white pillow. One long curl twisted enticingly
down over her breast, kissing the tempting curve. Rocco's
body was already hard. All it took was a look, or the memory of what it was like to surge into her tight, hot embrace.

He couldn't remember if he'd ever been with a lover so responsive and generous. He prided himself on being a virile, sensual man, and he enjoyed sex, but his experiences in recent years had all been…restrained. He'd found it easy not to lose control.

But all that had changed with Gracie. He cringed inwardly now to remember how he'd swept the things off the table in the kitchen so that he could take her there, as if he was some out of control rutting animal. And yet… she'd loved it. She'd splintered apart around him like his most secret erotic fantasy.

It was as if he'd been merely existing for a long time, and something or *someone* had woken him from a trance. Colours were more vivid, sounds sharper. Something fundamental in his beliefs about this woman had shifted last night when he'd seen how hard she'd worked to put together that beautiful meal. And when he'd seen the genuine hurt in her eyes at how she'd been spoken to. The fierce pride in her expression.

She'd spent the bare minimum on his credit card for the food. George had handed it back to him with an explicit look when he'd come back to the apartment before dinner, as if to say, *See? She's not like the rest.* And the assertion struck Rocco again that she didn't have anything to do with her brother's machinations. Even so—the voice of reason intruded—she was loyal to her brother, and that alone meant he couldn't fully trust her.

Rocco could feel the dominant part of himself that had struggled for so long to survive and attain his position try to assert itself. How could he be jeopardising so much, so easily, just for a woman? All his life he'd wanted to distance himself from drama and passion. Chaos and violence. The life he lived now was the absolute antithesis

of that. And he was considering diving back into it with
Gracie?

Yet surely all was not lost? He could have Gracie
O'Brien, and when this desire burnt itself out—as it always did—he would gather around the structures of his
life again and ensure his precious status once more.

He smiled cynically. Despite Honora Winthrop's dire
warning, he knew money could buy anything, and ultimately one of those women wouldn't be able to resist if
he wanted to enter into their protected society via marriage. Ever since that day in Italy when he'd been spat at
and ignored by his own blood family in the street, and he'd
watched them walk away, immune and protected by their
status, he'd craved that protection. That security. And he
could not lose sight of that now, when he had it in the palm
of his hand.

He could have it all, including Gracie, and he intended to.

Rocco walked back over to the bed and sat down, smiling when he saw a small frown pleat the smooth skin between her eyes. Her mouth was in a delicious moue, still
a little swollen. He bent and pressed a kiss there and her
eyes opened.

He drew back for a moment, to see her looking at him
with those wide, serious and wary eyes. Then she just said,
'Hi,' with a husky voice.

It was so simple and lacking in artifice that something
turned over in Rocco's chest. All his recent assertions suddenly felt very flimsy, and to avoid looking at *why* he just
bent his head and kissed Gracie until she was breathless
and arching her body into him and he lost himself in the
bliss of her again.

When Gracie woke she blinked and squinted against the
sun streaming into the bedroom. *Rocco's bedroom*. As

realisation sank in she squeezed her eyes tightly shut and groaned softly. And then she registered that she was naked and half uncovered. She scrabbled around for the sheet and pulled it right up over herself, and then peeped out to look around the room, trying to ignore the ache between her legs and in every muscle of her body.

The room was empty. All was still and quiet. She looked at the bedside clock and saw that it was one pm. With a squeal she sat up. And then lay back down again when she felt dizzy. Images started to flood her head. The endless night of being entangled with Rocco. His powerful body surging into hers over and over again, until she'd been weeping from an overdose of pleasure.

And then that morning, as dawn had broken outside, she'd woken to find him sitting there, just looking at her with such an intense expression, eyes dark. And he'd kissed her, and it had started all over again. Her body had been sensitive, but Gracie had loved the feel of Rocco moving so urgently within her.

But now when she moved a leg she winced. Sitting up again, Gracie cautiously got out of the bed, hugging the sheet around her, and went into the bathroom. Rocco's used towels lay on the floor and over the sink. His distinctive smell made her reel with a fresh onslaught of memories.

Gracie's brain shied away from trying to figure out how she could have given herself so freely to someone like him. He not only didn't trust her—he was a world away from her world. She came from an ugly council estate surrounded by grim flats and few opportunities. He came from a country steeped in beauty and undoubtedly from a lineage in which he could list his ancestors back as far as Caesar.

Gracie couldn't shower in his bathroom now. Not with his scent so fresh and mocking. She got to his bedroom door still with the sheet clasped around her and opened it quietly, half terrified she'd see him on the other side. No one was there. Gracie hurried back to her own room and shut and locked the door behind her.

And then she dived into her shower and scrubbed herself until her skin felt raw and sore muscles finally relaxed back to some semblance of normality. When she got out she dressed in loose pants and a shirt, as covered up as she could be. She tied her hair back into a ponytail.

When she opened her bedroom door she heard a noise coming from the kitchen and heat flooded her face when she thought of the carnage they'd left behind them. Her dress ripped open from neck to hem! Her discarded knickers!

Gracie imagined huge George in the middle of it, looking around with a scandalised expression, and with her face flaming she rushed to the kitchen. But the sight that greeted her was so unexpected that she stumbled to a halt. A small woman was mopping the floor, and the kitchen reflected nothing of the previous day or evening. Everything was tidied away, and fresh flowers stood on the table where Rocco and she had—

'You must be Gracie.'

Gracie looked stupidly at the middle-aged woman who was smiling and coming towards her with an outstretched hand.

Numbly Gracie shook her hand and nodded. 'Yes…I'm Gracie. I'm sorry, but…who are you?'

The woman smiled broadly. 'I'm Mrs Jones. I've been retained by Mr de Marco as his new housekeeper subject to a month's trial period.' She leaned on her mop and said conspiratorially, 'I've only just started back working full-time now that the kids are in college, so I don't know how it'll suit, but he seems nice…'

Gracie thought a little hysterically how *nice* didn't do him justice, and just looked at the woman who was chattering away as if nothing was wrong. If this woman was now the housekeeper, then what on earth was she?

'Are you all right, love?'

Gracie's focus came back to the housekeeper. Vaguely she nodded. 'Is George outside?'

The woman's eyes grew round. 'Is he the big man?'

Gracie nodded again and backed away, saying something about it being nice to meet her. She went out of the apartment to see George calmly reading a paper. He looked up and smiled. Gracie looked at him suspiciously. He didn't appear to be traumatised by anything he'd seen. Perhaps he'd not been into the kitchen?

She took a shaky breath. 'Do you know where Mr de Marco is?'

George frowned. 'He should be in his office. He went there a couple of hours ago, just after the new housekeeper arrived.'

Gracie nodded and made for the lift. She stopped when George called her name gently and turned around to follow his gaze—which was on her feet. Her *bare* feet. Smiling weakly, she went back inside to get some shoes.

Rocco was standing at his window. He ran a hand around the back of his neck. He couldn't ignore the steady hum of pleasure in his body, as if he'd just gorged on a feast. He grimaced. He *had*. A feast of Gracie.

His skin tightened imperceptibly and he stilled. He recognised instantly when the energy around the office changed. Slowly he turned around to see a pale-looking Gracie, covered from neck to toe in loose drab clothes, heading for his office. Her hair was tied back, making her look young. His gaze narrowed on her and with fatal predictability his body reacted. He regretted the countless glass windows and lack of privacy even more. And then his conscience struck him as he had a lurid image of what he'd like to do to her in his office. Gracie must be sore. She was so much smaller than him and she'd been so tight…

And yet she'd met him head-on every time, until exhaustion had finally claimed them both.

Gracie was almost at the door, her dark eyes on him with unwavering intensity in an unsmiling face. This was so far removed from any other morning-after situation he'd been in it was almost funny. But Rocco wasn't laughing when she walked in.

CHAPTER SEVEN

'WHAT's going on?' Gracie's arms were folded, as if that could help protect her from the sheer animal appeal of the man standing just a few feet away. Her body was betraying her, going into full on readiness mode. Nipples peaking, stomach tightening, and down below, between her legs…

'What are you talking about?'

Gracie willed her body to calm down and said tightly, 'I met the *new* housekeeper. So what does that make me?'

Rocco's hands were in his pockets. He wasn't wearing a jacket, just a shirt and tie, and he looked magnificent with the sun streaming in behind him, highlighting the broadness of his physique. His shirt was so finely made that she could see the dark hue of his skin and the delineated muscles.

He came around his desk then and perched on the corner, hands still in his pockets. For a moment Gracie had a rush of imagining that he had done that to stop himself from reaching for her, and cursed her runaway imagination.

'I hired Mrs Jones because I don't want you doing any more housework.'

Gracie injected false brightness into her voice. 'So I'm free to go?'

He shook his head, a glint in his eye. 'Not a chance.

You've never been less free.' There was a thrilling edge to his voice that made Gracie shiver and feel intense self-disgust at the same time.

'So...what? I've been promoted? To your bed?' She tried to make herself sound disgusted and scathing, but the words came out breathy.

A tiny smile turned up the corner of Rocco's mouth. 'Yes, you've been promoted to my bed. I like the sound of that.'

Feeling incredibly crabby all of a sudden, Gracie blurted out, 'Well, I don't. I'm not just a convenient plaything, you know.'

His mouth quirked. 'I am well aware of that. You're like a very volatile explosive substance mixed with the charm of a kitten and the claws of a big cat.'

Gracie blinked at him and said truthfully, 'I don't know if that's a compliment or an insult.'

'Oh, it's a compliment, believe me.' He stood up and came closer. Gracie's breath hitched. He cast a quick expressive glance either side of his office. 'You were right, you know...about the glass. It's so that I can see everyone at all times. It makes me nervous not to know who's coming or what's happening. But for once I wish I had blinds—or tinted windows.'

Gracie's throat went dry. She was mesmerised by the look in his eyes.

His voice was low and intimate, distracting Gracie from dwelling on his enigmatic words or their meaning. 'I'd lock the door so that I could take your hand and lead you over to the sofa. I'd pull you down and take off your top so that I could touch and taste your breasts. Then I would move my hand down, underneath the flimsy elastic of your trousers to your knickers. I would keep going until I could feel your soft curls. I wonder if they're already moistened—'

'Stop it!' Gracie all but hissed, arms clenched so tight across her chest that it was hard to breathe. She was sweating now, her heart beating rapidly, and down below… Lord, she wanted Rocco to pick her up and spread her across his desk the way he had in the kitchen last night.

She cast a quick mortified glance left and right. All she saw were bent industrious heads. She looked back to Rocco and felt dizzy. To anyone observing from the outside all they'd see was Rocco with his hands in his pockets, talking to the strange nondescript girl who'd suddenly started working for him.

But then Gracie looked down on an impulse and saw where his trousers were barely confining the truth of their conversation. She went puce.

In some pathetic effort to redirect the conversation she avoided Rocco's eye and asked, 'The kitchen…this morning…did Mrs Jones…?'

She couldn't finish—too mortified when she could see the carnage in her mind's eye again. She felt a finger come to her chin and Rocco tipped her face up. He'd moved closer, and she could smell heat and sex and lust. Her belly clenched tight with anticipation.

He shook his head. 'No. I cleared it up.'

Relief flooded Gracie even as she registered surprise. She said faintly, 'Somehow I can't see that happening.'

Rocco let her chin go and smiled dryly. 'I can pick things off the floor, you know. I'm not completely helpless.'

Gracie shivered. He wasn't helpless at all. He was like some magnificent urban animal. And then she thought of him picking up her knickers, and that dress that he'd ripped apart with his bare hands. With a muffled groan Gracie turned away to leave. Her head was churning, trying to make sense of where she stood now with Steven and everything, but she couldn't think when she was within three feet of this man.

She stopped when she heard Rocco say from behind her, 'Wait.'

Reluctantly she turned around again. He was standing behind his desk. She breathed a little easier.

'Do you have an up-to-date passport?'

She nodded, wondering where this was going.

'Good. In that case we're leaving this afternoon for Thailand for two days, and from there we'll go to New York for a couple of days.'

Gracie could hardly believe her ears. She shook her head slightly. 'Thailand?'

'It's a country in South-East Asia.'

'I know that,' she said impatiently, too afraid to believe this for a second. It had to be a joke. 'But…why?'

'Because I have to go on business and I want you to come with me.'

Her heart was thumping like a piston. 'As…what, exactly?'

He put his hands on his desk, spread wide. A feral look was in his eye and he smiled the smile of a consummate seducer. 'As my lover, of course.'

Gracie was still in a mild state of shock hours later, when she was in the back of Rocco's car with his long legs spread out beside her. She was clutching her passport in her hands and staring out of the window as London whizzed past and they entered countryside. Rocco's jet was at a private airfield. *Private jet.* Gracie felt a bubble of hysteria rising.

Suddenly her passport was taken out of her hands. Her head snapped around. 'Hey!'

She'd been avoiding looking at Rocco since he'd arrived back at the apartment to pick her up. He'd given her a scathing look up and down and muttered something about suitable clothes before making a call on his phone. Then he'd hustled her out of the apartment, leaving George behind, and into his car. And now he was perusing her passport. He looked up with an arched brow. 'You haven't travelled much?'

Gracie grabbed for her passport but Rocco held it aloft, and the motion of the car made her land awkwardly against his rock-hard torso. Cheeks flaming, Gracie scrabbled back, but Rocco snaked out an arm and captured her, holding her against him easily. Her breasts were crushed against him and her nipples were already peaking into tight stinging points.

Their faces were so close that Gracie could feel his warm breath. Her gaze slid to his mouth. She ached to touch it, to trace it with her finger. To feel the cushiony firmness.

Rocco's arm moved up and his hand speared into her hair, cradling the back of her head. 'Gracie…' he said roughly.

She ached for him to kiss her. The tension had been spiralling through her since she'd woken that morning, aching for him to touch her again. And she'd been in a state of near arousal since his provocative words in his office.

It was a few moments before either one of them heard the discreet knocking on the window beside Rocco. Gracie sprang apart from him, mortified by how ready she was for him to make love to her in the back of a car.

Gracie scrambled out, all but landing on the tarmac in an undignified heap. Rocco just looked at her with a bemused expression and Gracie scowled at him. She didn't need to suffer his look to know that he must be bemused by this attraction.

He set out across the tarmac to the plane, which was

glinting in the setting evening sun. Gracie stumbled slightly and Rocco stopped and held out a hand. She'd expected him to walk autocratically ahead of her, not even checking to see if she followed, and she looked at his hand for a long moment and then put her hand in his. His much bigger hand curled around hers, and her belly was swooping dangerously all the way to the plane with their fingers entwined.

For some reason, and she hated to admit this to herself, the moment felt significant.

Rocco looked at Gracie, sitting in a plush seat across the aisle from him. She was staring out of the window, fascinated, as if she'd never seen an airport before. He shook his head. This was a novelty for him: to be with a woman who didn't feel as if she had to give him her undivided attention and who also didn't seem to care one bit for the fact that she wore no make-up and such unflattering garments in front of her lover.

The few occasions he had ever taken a woman away with him for whatever reason had been like military operations, with an extra vehicle just to carry their luggage. He'd put up with it because he'd assured himself this was his world now, but he had to admit that it had always disgusted him a little bit.

He was getting irritated now by Gracie's extreme absorption in everything around her. The plane was starting to taxi down the runway and he spotted her open belt. That irritation laced his voice as he called to her, and something inside him clenched when he saw her flinch minutely before she turned her face to him.

He gestured to her lap. She looked down dumbly.

'Your safety belt.'

'Oh.' She found the two ends and clumsily tried to put them together.

Rocco had a flash of realisation when he remembered her brand spanking new passport. That something inside him clenched even tighter as he leaned across and made quick work of securing her belt, tightening it.

'I could have done it.'

Rocco sat back and looked at her. *Now* she was looking at him. 'You've never been on a plane before, have you?'

She flushed under his gaze. He could see her warring with the desire to blurt out, *Of course I have!* But after a moment she just shook her head, lips tight together. She was embarrassed, and Rocco's belly tightened with some nameless emotion.

He asked roughly, 'So why the brand-new passport? Were you planning on going somewhere?'

The second after he'd asked the question a cold trickle of realisation wound its way down his spine. His desire to trust her mocked him. How could he have been so stupid? Before Gracie could answer he laughed out loud. '*Dio.* Of course you were! You must have been planning a nice long overseas trip with your brother and the million euros he'd creamed off my clients.'

The mushy feelings Gracie had been feeling ever since Rocco had taken her hand dissolved. To think that she'd actually been about to tell him the real reason that she possessed a new passport! She cringed now at how he would have laughed at her.

Instead she tossed her head and smiled, drawing herself back deep inside and hating him for giving her such an amazing experience with one hand and then tainting it with the other.

'That's exactly it. We were thinking Australia, actually. A totally new and fresh start. Is that what you want to hear, Rocco? Because I can tell you what you want to hear until I'm blue in the face but it won't change the fact that it's not the truth.'

With that, she turned back to the window, drawing in a shaky breath. His inability to trust had taken her by surprise. It was as if once again she'd forgotten what lay between them. The inherent distrust and enmity. The waiting game until Steven came forward.

Steven. Abject guilt lanced her like a physical pain. How could she have not even thought about her brother? A lurid image from the previous night answered her question. She had no way of knowing now where he was or how he was, and for the first time she actually wanted Rocco's men to find him. Because at least that way she'd know he was safe and could then fight to protect him from Rocco's wrath. Also…Rocco would have no more reason to keep her as some sort of insurance. Because that was all this was to him: an indulgence, a convenient slaking of mutual desire.

As Gracie stared stonily out of the window, her hands clamping the armrests with a fear she refused to show at her very first take-off, she vowed not to let Rocco de Marco get under her skin, where he could do serious damage like all the other people in her life who'd hurt her. One by one they'd all left their indelible marks: her father, whom she barely remembered, her mother, grandmother, first boyfriend. She'd been abandoned or rejected by each and every one of them eventually. Steven was the only constant she'd ever known, and he needed her to be strong so that she could defend him again.

Ultimately Gracie could trust no one but herself, and the sooner she remembered that and stopped feeling things for Rocco de Marco that should never be given life the better.

* * *

An hour later Rocco sighed with frustration, spearing his hands through his hair. The tension between him and Gracie was thick enough to cut. And he couldn't stop feeling as if he'd done her some grievous injury. She was turned so resolutely towards the window that she was going to get a damned crick in her neck!

'Gracie...'

There was no reaction.

Rocco wasn't even sure what he wanted to say. Sorry? How could he be wanting to say sorry and believe in her innocence when he had every reason to believe that she would be firmly on the side of her brother? He'd seen the photo of them as kids; they were as thick as thieves. Why else would she have a brand-new passport...?

He looked more closely at Gracie now and saw that she was breathing steadily. But she looked extremely uncomfortable. Because she was hell-bent on avoiding him? Her words came back to him accusingly: *'I can tell you what you want to hear until I'm blue in the face but it won't change the fact that it's not the truth.'* Cursing softly, he put aside the papers that he'd been failing miserably to concentrate on anyway and got out of his seat.

He bent over Gracie to see her pale cheeks. She was asleep. Lashes, long and dark, highlighted the translucence of her skin. And everything in him stilled when he saw the distinctive salty track of a tear down one cheek. His belly clenched hard. *She'd been crying.*

Cursing more volubly now, Rocco undid Gracie's belt and scooped her up out of the chair. She came awake groggily in his arms as he made his way down the centre of the plane, moving against his chest, making his blood go hot when he felt her soft breasts.

'Shh, you fell asleep. I'm just going to make you more comfortable.'

Gracie was too sleepy to come out of it completely. And she didn't want to—not when she felt so secure and safe with Rocco's arms around her. She knew she should be fighting *something*, but she couldn't drum up the energy to figure out what, exactly, and she didn't want to look at why she felt the remnants of anger at Rocco.

She felt herself being lowered down onto a soft surface, and then something deliciously silky being lifted over her. Her shoes were being removed. And then the bed dipped and she felt the slightest touch to her forehead. So light she wasn't even sure if it was a kiss.

Much later Gracie woke up, completely disorientated, with a strange sound in her ears. She slowly came round and realised the sound was the relentless hum of the plane. She looked around the dimly lit room, her mouth opening. She was in a *bedroom*, on a *plane*.

She put back the cover and padded over to one of the porthole windows and looked out. She could see bright sunlight, the curvature of the earth, and down far below majestic white-capped mountains. She'd never seen anything so spectacular.

She stood up and stretched, and tried to piece together how she'd come to be lying in the bed. She remembered being in Rocco's arms. And a kiss? She frowned. Perhaps it had just been a dream?

Her hurt at his blatant mistrust seemed to have faded. Logically Gracie knew that there was no way he'd ever really trust her. Her brother was missing with a million euros and she looked guilty as hell because she'd gone looking for him. And she insisted on defending him when even she had to concede that he had to be guilty.

She shut off her brain from wishing things could be different and explored the bedroom. She found an *en suite* bathroom, complete with fluffy towels and a bath and shower. Stocked to the brim with toiletries. Feeling sticky and gritty, she took the opportunity and stripped down to step into a steaming shower. She couldn't get her head around the fact that she was having a shower thousands of feet in the air and smiled gleefully, choosing for a blissful moment to forget what lay beyond the doors.

When she emerged back into the bedroom with a towel wrapped around her body she spotted numerous shopping bags and boxes. Unable to help investigating, she saw that they were all women's clothes. *For her?*

She quickly dressed, in her own jeans and a fresh shirt from her own suitcase, and went to find Rocco. When she opened the door, though, the plane was quiet and still dimly lit. There'd only been one flight attendant when they'd embarked—a man—and Gracie imagined he must be sleeping somewhere too.

She couldn't see Rocco's head, and crept up the aisle—only to come to a halt when she could see that his seat was back as far as it would go and he was asleep. Guilt spiked her, because he couldn't be as comfortable as she'd been in the bed.

One arm was flung up; the other rested over his chest. He looked so much younger that she sat down on the arm of the seat opposite and let her eyes rove over his face. He looked so much more approachable when in repose, and she had a sudden aching desire to know what it would be like to see him really relaxed, without that brooding intensity or that constant sardonic smile.

Suddenly he shifted and Gracie sprang up, aghast at the thought of being found staring at him like some lovestruck groupie. She was glancing left and right before she looked down again and saw him coming awake. Still managing to look gorgeous and not half as bleary as she felt.

'I'm sorry. I didn't meant to wake you.' To Gracie's surprise Rocco looked uncharacteristically disorientated. She was so used to seeing him in full control at all times this was like seeing a chink in his armour, and it made her heart turn over. And then she remembered his caustic comments and felt hurt all over again.

Before she could do anything, though, he'd recovered his composure with lightning speed and reached out to catch her wrist, pulling her off balance so she fell on top of him. She squealed and landed breathless on his wide chest. He had his hands on her waist and they were burrowing under her shirt to find her skin. His eyes were dark and heavy-lidded from sleep.

Gracie squirmed and felt heat rush to every extremity. 'Rocco…stop.' The words came out breathy and carried absolutely no conviction whatsoever. Her hurt at his suspicion of her was draining away. She was officially weak and shallow.

And then his hands did stop. He looked at her for a long moment and asked in a rough-sounding voice, 'So why *do* you have a brand-new passport, then?'

Gracie held her breath for a long moment, eyes searching his face for some sign he wasn't taking her seriously. She let out her breath and said a little shakily, 'You'll laugh at me.'

'Try me.'

Gracie tried to pull back but Rocco only snaked his hands tighter around her, so that she was all but welded to his chest and her bottom sat snugly in his lap. How was she supposed to concentrate when she could feel him hardening against her?

She looked down, avoiding his eyes, as if that could help her concentrate, and played with a button on his shirt. She took a breath.

'The reason I have a brand-new passport is because ever since I was little I always wanted to travel. I got a passport as soon as I could, even though I had no intention of going anywhere, and it was renewed just recently. I just liked the idea of having one, so I'd be ready to leave at a moment's notice…it seemed romantic to me—like there was this world of opportunity I could explore some day.' Gracie snuck a quick glance at Rocco and couldn't decipher his stony expression. She'd never felt so exposed, and looked down again. 'It's silly, I know…'

Rocco battled hard against the maelstrom inside him. Either Gracie was the best actress on the planet…or she was telling the truth. She couldn't even look him in the eye and his heart twisted. He knew what she was talking about, because the moment he'd taken his first passport in his hand he too had felt that sense of opportunity open up before him. He'd left Italy and never looked back.

He put a hand to her chin and tipped her face up to his, valiantly trying to screen the emotion he felt with the only weapon in his possession. Passion. Softly, though, before he gave in to it weakly, he just said, 'Okay.'

Gracie looked at him. 'Okay?'

Gruffly now, he said, 'I believe you.'

Gracie's heart felt as if it was expanding in her chest. All her hurt and anger dissolved and silently she cursed Rocco, perversely knowing that if he'd insisted on not believing her she would find it so much easier to deal with him.

He stood up then, taking her with him in his arms, and she squealed again. As he brought her towards the bedroom and her skin prickled with anticipation, she said breathlessly, 'Where are we going?'

'To join the mile-high club.'

Gracie's insides liquified. '*Rocco*…we can't…'

But her plaintive plea was cut off by the closing door, and when Rocco put her down and put his hands around her face and kissed her senseless she couldn't think of one reason why they couldn't.

An hour later Gracie was draped over Rocco's big body, legs either side of his hips. Their breathing was still erratic, hearts thumping hard. She'd hoped that making love wouldn't be as intense as the first time, but it had been even more intense. Because now her body knew the pleasure he could give her.

She was a mere novice when it came to sex, but in the space of twenty-four hours she felt as if she'd been spoilt for life. She knew instinctively that no other man could affect her like Rocco did. Lightning didn't strike twice. Her heart twisted ominously when she considered that the experience for him must be so much more banal.

Her hand was on his shoulder, and as she moved it down she felt some puckered skin. She lifted her head to look and saw some kind of scar. She'd never noticed it before. She touched it with a finger, tracing the outline, and could feel Rocco tense.

'What's this?' she asked.

His chest moved. 'I fell off my bike when I was a child.'

Gracie looked at him suspiciously. His eyes were still closed and she'd bet money that that was a lie. It had come out far too glibly. But why would he lie?

Knowing that he would be as likely to open up to her as he would to forgive Steven for his crime, she veered away from danger and said instead, 'When I woke up first we were flying over snow-capped mountains. What were they?'

'It was most likely the Himalayas.'

'Wow...' Gracie breathed. Feeling a little emotional, she said, 'I can't believe I might have been looking at Everest.'

Rocco shrugged minutely and said, 'Could have been.'

He opened sleepy eyes and his vaguely bored tone affected Gracie. She half slithered, half climbed off his body and looked at him 'You don't have a clue how privileged you are, do you? Is it really so easy to take everything for granted?'

She stood up from the bed, self-conscious in her nudity, and looked around for her clothes. But her wrist was grabbed and she was pulled back down. Rocco's eyes were dark and unreadable.

'I don't take it for granted,' he bit out. 'Not one second of it.'

The quality of his voice made Gracie go still. She'd touched a nerve, and she was reminded of that cataclysmic night in the kitchen when he'd told her he knew what it was like to not be noticed.

'It's just...it doesn't seem that way. You have the best of everything. Expect the best without question.'

'Because I can. Because I've earned it. What do you care anyway?'

What do you care? That question sent shards of fear through her. Why did it matter so much? Gracie looked at him and tried in vain to read his expression. He was so closed. She cared because she just *knew* there was something more to this man than the surface desire to be successful and surround himself with the trappings of the truly rich. There was a darker vein. She'd always sensed it.

There was a long, enigmatic silence and Gracie held her breath. For a moment she felt sure that Rocco was going to say something, but then he moved his hand from around her wrist, up her arm and around her neck to pull her down. He pressed a kiss to her mouth, making her open up to him.

After an intoxicating few seconds Gracie could feel herself tumbling headlong back towards ecstasy. It was like standing on the edge of a huge chasm with nothing to hold onto when she started to fall. She was terrified Rocco would see how much control over her he had.

She pulled back and he smiled at her lazily, his hand making circles on her back. He was turning on the charm, and she cursed him because it worked. When he smiled like that all she wanted to do was purr like a kitten.

Clearly he was avoiding any more probing questions.

She pulled away more forcefully this time and sat up. 'I'm going to take a shower.'

She stood up and walked over to the bathroom with as much insouciance as she could muster, desperately aware of Rocco's eyes burning into her back.

As soon as Gracie had disappeared into the bathroom the smile slid from Rocco's face. He lay back in the bed, his whole body tense, hands clenched to fists over the sheet which barely covered him. He cursed himself and called himself all sorts of names. Gracie had a unique ability to push his buttons and he couldn't help lashing out. He'd nearly smacked her hand away when she'd touched the scar from his old tattoo. Sleeping with her again had flayed him alive from the inside out. It was as if she could see right into where he was a fake. Where the thin veneer over his life was so flimsy it might fall away at any moment, exposing him.

He had not expected to feel that same out-of-control animalistic urge again. He'd imagined the edge would be gone from his need. But as soon as he'd had Gracie's face in his hands and her mouth under his all he'd been able to remember was the urgent need to fuse with her. The plane could have gone down into Everest and he wouldn't have noticed or cared.

And she'd met him every step of the way—even more explosively now than the first time. Rocco cursed out loud. Women did *not* get under his skin like this. His mother had taught him his first lesson by never putting him first. Whoever had been her current benefactor, or her pimp, had always been number one.

As a hormonal teenager Rocco had found that the girls he'd made a fool of himself over went with the boys with the biggest guns, the most swagger. To this day he gave thanks that he hadn't joined their ranks just to get a girl who would have soon dumped him for the next big thing. That had been his second big lesson.

His third had been when his sisters—two beautiful blonde, blue-eyed princesses—had stepped over him in the street without so much as a flicker of interest in the young man who had just confronted *their* papa, calling him *Father*. They'd not even flinched when their father had spat at him and pushed him to the ground.

When Rocco had finally left Italy and clawed his way up the ladder he'd taken great pleasure in seducing women from that world. Women who were privileged. There had been a measure of satisfaction in knowing that they would never touch an icy-cold and unbreakable part of him. The colder he was, the more he gained a reputation and a slavish following. His greatest satisfaction had come from imagining the horror and recoil on their faces if they really knew his darkest past.

But Gracie, with her serious eyes, her fierce protectiveness of her brother, and her slightly choked awe at flying over the Himalayas was fast unravelling what felt like years of block-building. He'd had no defences to pull around himself when she'd told him about the passport. Nowhere to go to hide or attack, which was what he was used to doing when he felt vulnerable.

She was connecting to a part of him long buried and denied, and he didn't like the lack of equilibrium that came with that. Rocco knew he'd be the biggest fool to believe in the track of a tear on a woman's cheek, or a cute story about a childhood dream, and yet—for possibly the first time in his life—he found a part of himself wanted to believe. Even just for a moment.

CHAPTER EIGHT

'Who are the clothes for?' Gracie asked when she stepped out of the bathroom for a second time in a towel. The sun was high now outside, and she could see brown earth far below. She felt a shiver of excitement.

Rocco must have showered in another bathroom as he was just finishing buttoning up a shirt, hair damp and looking dynamic and virile. He looked at her. 'They're for you.'

Gracie felt herself grow tense. 'But I have clothes.'

'You need suitable clothes for the weather. You have no idea how hot it's going to be. Also, I'm due to attend some functions in Bangkok and New York, so you'll need appropriate evening dress.'

Gracie bit her lip and looked at the bags warily. 'It feels weird, I don't want you dressing me.'

Rocco looked impatient now. 'It's no big deal. Luckily I realised in time.'

Fire flashed up Gracie's spine and she put her hands on her hips. 'Oh? Because you're afraid I'd embarrass you in public? Perhaps you shouldn't have been so hasty kicking your fiancée out the other night. You wouldn't have to dress *her*.'

Gracie knew she sounded petulant but she couldn't seem to stop. The contrast between her and Rocco's usual women was stark right now, and clearly she didn't measure up.

'Need I remind you that the outfit you made me wear the other evening was a size too small? But if you don't mind me parading around with my—'

'Enough!'

Gracie shut her mouth.

Rocco prowled closer and Gracie gulped. He looked dangerous. She could see a muscle throb in his jaw.

'For the umpteenth time, she was *not* my fiancée. And the company that sent the serving dress made an error on the size. I think you'll find that these will be a perfect fit, and if you don't put them on I *will* dress you myself.'

Gracie stuck up her chin. 'You don't scare me, you know.'

For a second he didn't react, and then Rocco laughed out loud, head thrown back. He looked back at her, eyes glinting and took her breath away.

'I know,' he said, with a peculiar quality to his voice. 'Believe me, you're the only one.'

When Rocco had walked out to let Gracie dress, she sucked in a deep quivery breath. The intensity of their lovemaking was still making her feel rawly vulnerable. She cursed herself for her reaction just now. The last thing she needed was that far too probing brain of his investigating why he pushed her buttons. She explored the bags of clothes and saw that they *were* the right size. Rocco had thought of everything—even make-up.

Reluctantly she packed away her own jeans and shabby shirt and, feeling like a fraud, dressed in a silk shirt, tailored lightweight linen trousers and flat shoes, and tried not to like how amazing the expensive fabrics felt against her skin.

* * *

A little later Gracie was sitting back in her seat with the belt buckled, barely able to contain her excitement as the plane descended through stormy-looking clouds into Bangkok.

The plane suddenly dipped and Gracie gripped her seat, looking at Rocco with panic. 'What was that?'

'Turbulence. It's rainy season in Bangkok, so it'll be stormy, but the rain is warm.'

'Warm?' Gracie knew she must sound ridiculous, but Rocco was reaching across the aisle for her.

'Come here,' he said throatily.

She scrambled out of her seat, more nervous than she cared to admit, and he swapped seats so that she could sit beside him at the window. She looked at him. 'But you won't be able to see.'

He gave her a funny look before replying, 'I've seen it before. It's your first time.'

Gracie finally tore her eyes away and looked down. They were just breaking through the clouds and she gasped in awe at the land below. 'It's so green. I never thought it would be so green!'

Rocco had his arms around her and his head close to hers. 'It's a mixture of jungle and paddy fields...rice paddies. It's quite a lush country—especially in the rainy season.'

Gracie was shaking her head in awe, drinking it in. She could see a huge distinctively shaped temple right in the middle of a field, with tiny stick insect people walking back and forth. 'It's so beautiful.'

Rocco's voice was amused. 'You haven't even seen it yet. Not properly.'

She turned her head. 'Will there be time...I mean, to look around?'

Rocco felt that tightness in his chest as he looked into

those brown gold-flecked eyes. He nodded. 'Sure. We can go to the Grand Palace, and see some other things too.'

Impulsively Gracie pressed a kiss to Rocco's mouth, and then turned away quickly before he could see the surge of emotion she was feeling on her face.

Gracie was still reeling from the terror of her first plane landing and the intensity of the damp heat when they'd walked out of the plane about thirty minutes ago. The sheer force of heat had hit her and instantly made her feel as overdressed as someone in a ski-suit.

Rocco had looked at her when they'd got into the back of a gloriously air-conditioned car, arched a brow and drawled laconically, 'I told you so.'

Even in the space of those few minutes between plane and car Gracie's shirt had begun sticking to her and her hair had started frizzing up. Rocco looked as unfazed as ever, and Gracie stuck her tongue out at him. 'Does nothing ever affect you?'

Rocco's face went serious and his eyes darkened as he drawled, 'You do a pretty good job of affecting me.'

Gracie tore her gaze from Rocco's with an effort. She was still freaked out by how quickly she lost control around him. Luckily they were soon smack-bang in the middle of Bangkok, and that sucked up all her attention.

The roads were wide, and tall skyscrapers pierced grey skies. It was all at once hectic and modern and ancient. Huge billboards written in a fascinating script showed pictures of gorgeous Thai families. Horns were screeching and there seemed to be a million mopeds, some of them carrying what looked like entire families. Serene-looking women were perched on the back seat, side-saddle-style, with babies in laps and helmets over their veils. Gracie's eyes were huge as she took it all in.

She pointed at something. 'What are they?'

Rocco followed her gaze and said, 'They're called Tuk-Tuks. They're motorised rickshaws used as taxis.'

Gracie looked after the little vehicles wistfully, before her attention was taken by something else. Rocco stared at her face, enraptured by all her expressions, before he realised and broke his gaze away. He cursed himself. He had occasionally brought women on business trips, especially if he needed a companion for the ubiquitous social engagements. But he knew well that he'd never been so effortlessly distracted before.

He could well imagine the blasé reaction of someone like Honora Winthrop to Bangkok. Some people hated it, but it was one of Rocco's favourite cities and he couldn't help the warm feeling at seeing that Gracie looked as if she was going to love it too.

When they arrived at the hotel Gracie scrambled out of the car before the driver could open the door. She was like an irrepressible puppy. She turned around to face Rocco, a huge smile on her face. 'I *love* this heat. It's like standing in a warm shower after the water has stopped. And the smells are so exotic…'

Rocco tried not to notice how the silk of her shirt was already damp with her body heat and clung to her breasts, outlining their firm shape, the thrust of her nipples. The new clothes hugged her lithe figure, attracting attention, making him suddenly wish she was still dressed in her plain clothes.

He gritted his jaw and took her arm to lead her into the most exclusive hotel in Bangkok. It was one of the prestigious Wolfe chain of hotels, and he knew Sebastian Wolfe, the owner, personally. When they were on their way up in the lift Rocco looked at Gracie. He found that he was already anticipating her reaction to the room. And when the manager showed them in he wasn't disappointed.

Gracie walked around, speechless. She touched the backs of chairs and ran her hand along gleaming table tops. She found sliding doors and opened them, to step out onto a huge terrace which overlooked the Chao Praya river.

Rocco put down his laptop case and strolled towards the doors. The manager had left, after assuring Rocco fervently that he must call him any time of day or night if he needed anything. Rocco smiled. He didn't doubt that he had been personally informed by Sebastian to take care of him.

Rocco was reminded for a minute that Sebastian had recently married his beautiful Indian wife, and only a few weeks later she'd given birth to their baby boy. Sebastian had sent Rocco a picture of the three of them together, and it was an image of family bliss that Rocco had found almost difficult to look at. He pushed the memory aside now, frowning when he couldn't see Gracie.

Suddenly she appeared from around the corner, where a huge bamboo tree swayed gently in the breeze. 'There's a *pool*! Our very own private pool.'

He smiled and put his hands in his pockets, because he didn't think he'd be able to stop himself from touching her. 'I know.'

Her face fell, and it had an instant effect on his mood. 'Oh, of course you do. You must have been here a thousand times before.'

He gave up the effort it took to restrain himself and walked over, hating her crestfallen expression. He put an arm around her, pulling her close, and tipped her chin up. 'Not quite a thousand…a lot of times, though. You like it here?'

Gracie smiled and looked embarrassed, 'Like it? Are you crazy? This place is like Eden. I've never seen anything like it. The city is…overwhelming, breathtaking. This hotel is like…another world.'

Rocco pulled her closer and spoke without thinking. '*You're* breathtaking.'

Gracie's cheeks went a delicate pink, and she buried her head in his chest and mumbled, 'No, I'm not.' She looked up then. 'I'm just normal, and I think that's a novelty for you.'

His heart clenched. If only she knew. He lifted up a hand and kissed it, noticing that her palms had already started to soften. The realisation forced him to make his voice sound light. 'I have to meet with some clients downstairs. Why don't you have a nap and settle in? The jet lag shouldn't be too bad as we slept on the plane. We're going out tonight to a function, and then I'll be at meetings most of the day tomorrow.'

Gracie just nodded, out of her depth in more ways than one. His words sank in—one in particular. *Function.* She bit her lip.

'The function tonight…will it be very grand?'

Rocco nodded, with a serious expression on his face. 'It'll be disgustingly grand, and there's going to be a huge buffet—so you'd better bring a suitcase to fill for any needy neighbours.'

It took a second for Gracie to realise he was making fun of her. She mock-hit him, but trembled inside at his easy humour. Lord, when he turned on the charm he needed to come with a health warning.

'Seriously, though, I've only ever been to that one in London. What if people talk to me?'

'Talk back.' He quirked a dry smile. 'You didn't seem

to have a problem talking to me that night. Just don't assume everyone's security.'

And then he was letting her go and stepping away. Gracie felt ridiculously insecure, but kept her hands by her sides.

'I'll see you in a few hours.' And then he'd turned and was striding away with that mesmeric athletic grace.

That evening Gracie gave herself a last once-over. Rocco was waiting outside, in one of the suite's main lounges. They each had their own bathrooms and dressing rooms. She still couldn't take in the opulence of it all. Everything was dark wood and dimly lit. Asian antiquities were lit up in artful cubbyholes by spotlights. Gorgeous ornate silk coverings and cushions littered the sumptuous furniture and bedroom. The bathroom had two showers—one was open to the elements. The bed in their room alone would have slept a football team comfortably.

Inside the suite was almost cold with the air-conditioning, and when she stepped outside it was like stepping into a warm oven.

She took a deep breath. The dress she wore shimmered with a million varying shades of red and burnt orange. It should have clashed with her colouring, but it didn't. Made of some kind of delicate lamé material, it fell to the floor in a swirl of different colours. It was V-necked and sleeveless. Gracie looked very pale. She felt so insecure about what she should wear, but how could she ask Rocco for advice? He was a man. She should *know* these things.

She wore high-heeled strappy red sandals, and she'd made an effort with make-up. She'd dithered with her hair for ages and had finally managed to tame it into a chignon. Taking another deep breath, she turned away and picked up a small gold clutch bag. She walked out slowly in the heels, and saw Rocco standing at the now closed sliding doors. His hands were in his pockets and his back looked impossibly broad in the black suit. Hair curling a touch over his collar, exactly as she'd noticed that first night in London.

For a heart-stopping moment Gracie had an overwhelming instinct to run far away and fast. But at the same moment he must have heard her, and turned to look around. His eyes dropped and then came back up, widening imperceptibly.

Worried, she asked huskily, 'Is it okay? I wasn't sure what would be appropriate—'

'It's perfect.'

He came towards her then, hands coming out of his trouser pockets, and Gracie almost stumbled backwards at the sheer force of him in the tuxedo. She was standing by a table and he reached down and picked up a box she hadn't noticed. He opened it up, presenting it to her, and she looked down to see a plain diamond studded necklace and stunning diamond drop earrings.

She looked up at him. 'What's this?'

He frowned. 'Jewellery for you to wear.'

Gracie shook her head, backing away a little. 'It's too much, Rocco. I can't wear these. They must be worth a fortune.'

A dark shadow seemed to pass over his face, and then it cleared. Easily he said, 'They're from the shop in the hotel. They can be returned in the morning.'

She looked at him suspiciously. 'They're really only for tonight?'

He nodded, his eyes unreadable. 'If you want.'

Gracie looked at the jewels again, and after a long second nodded. 'Okay. I'll wear them.'

Rocco took out the necklace and deftly fastened it around her neck. Then he handed her the earrings. She put them in with shaky hands. The necklace felt cool and heavy around her throat, and the earrings swung when she moved her head.

Rocco held out an arm and said, 'Shall we?'

Gracie nodded and put her arm in his, and felt ridiculously as if she were walking to some kind of gallows.

Rocco kept Gracie's arm firmly in his. He could feel the tiny tremors in her body as they went down in the lift. She was *nervous*. In the reflection of the lift doors she almost looked a little ill. And despite that she looked stunning. When she'd emerged from the bedroom for a split second he hadn't recognised her. Her hair up showed off her long graceful neck. Make-up made her cheeks dewy, her eyes even bigger, lashes so long he'd seen them from across the room.

The colours of the dress shimmered around her like a hundred exotic birds, and the way the material clung to her curves showed off her petite lithe physique to perfection. With the tiniest amount of polish she had morphed into a beauty who could give any woman in his sphere a run for her money.

The diamonds were picking up the colours of her dress and flashed like fire around her neck and ears. He was so used to the routine of buying women jewellery when he took them out like this that he'd not been prepared for Gracie's reaction, and he didn't like the way it added to the clamour in his head urging him to believe in her innocence. The feeling of claustrophobia was back, but this time for entirely different reasons.

They travelled the short distance to where the function was being held in the chauffeur-driven limousine which had picked them up from the airport. When they stepped out of the car Gracie relished the warm, sultry blanket of air. Rocco was leading her into a beautifully ornate wooden building, its lines long and swooping in the distinctive Thai style. It was all so impossibly foreign. Like nothing she'd ever seen before. Gracie was drunk on the sights and smells, and the fascinatingly staccato sounds of the Thai language.

The building was open to the elements on all sides and surrounded by stunning gardens where the trees were lit up with fairy lights, giving everything a magical air. The rain had stopped and stars lit up the sky. Beautiful Thai women moved through the crowd in traditional long skirts, serving drinks and food.

Gracie refused a glass of champagne and Rocco replaced it with water, saying easily, 'You don't drink at all?'

Gracie grimaced and avoided his eye. 'My mother was an alcoholic—and my grandmother. I've never touched the stuff.'

He looked at her for a long moment. She glanced at him quickly and then away again.

She couldn't believe she'd just told him that so easily, and spoke again to distract him. 'The women are so petite. I feel like an elephant next to them.'

Rocco took her free hand and lifted it to his mouth. Gracie looked up and her breath caught when he kissed the inner palm. 'You do *not* look like an elephant. You look stunning.'

'Th-thank you,' Gracie stuttered. She couldn't really believe she was here. In this dress. With Rocco de Marco. It was as if the fantasy she'd indulged in after they'd met for the first time had been plucked out of her brain and made real. It was too much.

She knew rationally that he was only being charming because she was there to fulfil a function in his bed, because he desired her momentarily, but she couldn't help her silly heart from thumping ominously. Her mind was screaming, *Danger, danger.* Especially after what had happened on the plane, when he'd shown his deep mistrust of her. But then he'd dissolved that anger by asking her to explain about the passport. She cursed him again silently for removing her defences as though they were mere children's play-blocks.

Rocco led her further into the crowd, through the main room and out to where tables dotted the gardens, candles flickering like small beacons of light. Gracie was glad Rocco had thought to give her some mosquito repellent earlier. She could well imagine that her whiter than white skin would be a magnet on a night like tonight.

Just then a man approached Rocco and clapped him heartily on the back, and that was the start of a long evening during which people approached Rocco and talked to him about things Gracie had never heard of nor could understand. Things like market forces and trends. But she didn't mind. She'd always found it fascinating just to listen to other people talk.

'Are you bored?'

Gracie looked up at Rocco, genuinely shocked. Another man had just walked away. 'No! Why? Did you think I was?'

'No,' he said dryly. 'But you're awfully quiet and that makes me nervous.'

She shrugged. 'I don't have a clue what you're talking about most of the time.' Then she smiled. 'I would have thought that was a welcome relief.'

Rocco quirked a smile. 'Strangely enough, not as much as I would have expected.' He faced her fully then, and asked, 'That folder in your case, with the sketchings and text…what is it?'

Gracie flushed and her heart constricted. Reality intruded on the halcyon moment, reminding her why she was there. 'I should have known you'd looked at that too. Did you expect to find plans for a bank raid?'

She looked away, and then back when Rocco caught her chin with his fingers. He actually looked uncomfortable for a moment.

'I might have suspected finding something like that before…but now I don't know…'

Something inside Gracie swooped dangerously. She took a breath, and a leap into this very tenuous evidence of Rocco's trust before it disappeared. 'I did a basic art degree. I want to write children's books some day. It's just a few sketches and ideas. Nothing special.'

'I thought they looked pretty good.'

Gracie looked at him, a curious melting feeling in her chest. 'Really?'

He nodded. Gracie's heart kicked once, hard. He took his hand from her chin.

'What made you want to write children's books?'

Gracie's hands played with her bag. She'd never really told anyone this before and felt ridiculously exposed. 'I was never very good at school…not like—' She stopped herself from saying *Steven*, not wanting to jeopardise the fragile truce that seemed to exist between her and Rocco now. 'Not like most of the other kids… I always loved reading and books—the way they could they could transport you into another world.' She shrugged now, feeling silly, and avoided Rocco's piercing black gaze. 'It struck a chord and I wanted to recreate that.'

Rocco looked at Gracie's downbent head. Her hair shone like gold fire. He could imagine only too well how tantalising it must have been to lose herself in stories and magic as a child when she'd been living in such an inconstant world.

Rocco said nothing and Gracie looked up, nearly taking a step backwards at the intensity of his expression. She quickly became transfixed by his mouth, wanting to relax it from the taut line it had become.

'Don't look at me like that,' he growled.

'Or what?' Gracie asked, suddenly feeling confident in a way she never had before. It was a confidence that came from Rocco not laughing at her ambition and from being *desired*.

'Or I'll take you out of here right now and do something about it.'

Gracie looked up at him, feeling bold. 'I'm not stopping you.'

With a half-muttered curse Gracie felt her hand being taken in Rocco's and she was being led back through the throng. She felt buoyant that she could have this singular effect on Rocco. She felt buoyant with this growing ease between them.

Within minutes they were in the back of his car, the privacy window was up, and Gracie turned unquestioningly into Rocco's arms, her mouth searching desperately for his…

A short while later, when they got into the lift back at the hotel, Rocco could see Gracie's face, pink with embarrassment, reflected in the steel surface. She'd stopped him just as he'd been stepping from the car and whispered, 'They'll *know*.'

Her hair was down and dishevelled, her mouth swollen. And her hand was clasped tight in his. He'd almost taken her in the back seat of the car, a simple kiss having exploded into something much hotter within seconds.

Gracie's eyes were downcast, and he had to curb the concern he felt. He was struggling to rein in anger mixed with desire. He didn't *do* this. He didn't become so transfixed with a woman that he left functions early. And he didn't make love to women in the backs of cars. It was as if any enclosed space automatically became a provocation, an enticement to seduce her.

Only the tiniest sliver of sanity was preventing him from hitting the *Stop* button in the lift so he could hike up that dress and touch her. And also the knowledge that his friend Sebastian would not appreciate the X-rated CCTV elevator show.

When they reached the penthouse suite Gracie moved skittishly away, taking her hand out of his. Rocco's body throbbed to continue what they'd started.

He saw her hands go to the necklace. He frowned. 'What are you doing?'

'I want to take this off.'

She sounded breathless and husky and vulnerable all at once, and Rocco's chest tightened. Maybe he wasn't the only one feeling off-kilter because of this insatiable desire.

He stepped forward and gritted his teeth as her scent, musky with arousal, hit his nostrils. He told himself harshly that he could control himself. He took off the necklace and she handed him the earrings too.

She was looking around, still avoiding his eye. 'We should put them in the safe or something.'

Rocco sighed with impatience at her pragmatism, but duly found the box and put the jewellery in the suite's safe. As he went back out to the living area he yanked off his bow tie and shed his jacket. Gracie had disappeared, but the sliding doors were open. He went out. She was standing at the edge of the shimmering pool in her bare feet, shoes tumbled nearby.

Her dress glittered against the dusky night sky, her skin glowed like a pearl, and he felt as if he was falling.

* * *

Gracie heard Rocco's footfall behind her. She finally felt a little more in control. As they'd walked through the hotel lobby she'd felt as if everyone could see her shame all over her skin. *How* had she morphed into this person who felt confident enough to entice Rocco away from a party and then jump on him in the back of his car like a sex-starved groupie?

In the lift on the way up to the suite she'd been so hungry for him that she'd ached for him to stop the lift and take her right there, with her dress pushed up around her waist and her knickers ripped off.

The strength of her desire had shocked her so much that she'd felt as if she might break apart if Rocco touched her as soon as they got into the apartment. She'd focused on the jewellery to stall him, even for a moment, too embarrassed even to look at him.

Rocco was standing beside her now and she glanced at him, feeling shy all of a sudden. He was looking down at the water.

She wondered if he felt overwhelmed by this intensity too, and then had to berate herself. Rocco wouldn't feel overwhelmed by anything.

She spoke to break the tense silence. 'The air feels denser...more humid.'

Rocco glanced up at the sky. 'A storm is about to hit. The rain will start again any minute now.'

Gracie looked up and saw threatening clouds overhead. She heard the clap of thunder and flinched minutely. 'Is it really warm when it falls?'

'Yes.'

Gracie felt as if her nerve-endings were exposed. She took a breath and turned towards Rocco. 'What happened back there...at the function...and in the car. It scares me a little—the way things escalate so fast between us.'

The air went still around them, and another distant clap of thunder came.

Rocco said carefully, without looking at her, 'What do you mean?'

Gracie shrugged and turned back to curl her bare unvarnished toes over the edge of the pool. She looked down. 'I'm not sure. I just…I want you to know that I don't…I've never felt like this before.'

She felt him turn towards her and looked up. He seemed angry.

'You think this is normal for me? This…insane desire?'

Hurt lanced Gracie. 'I don't think it's insane. It's just… it feels like it's not entirely in our control…'

'You've got that right,' he said broodingly, and looked away again.

Something clicked into place and Gracie felt as if she had just stumbled on something that was fundamentally a part of Rocco's psyche. She could sense the wildness in him that he denied, and how much he hated not being in control of it; much the same thing scared her. But he really resented it. She only had to remember the icy-cool beauty of Honora Winthrop to know which he would ultimately prefer. Gracie was a mere indulgence in his dark side.

Gracie looked back at the placid surface of the water and felt Rocco's crackling tension beside her. That placid surface seemed to mock her now. A flicker of rebellion at Rocco's evident distaste of this lack of control came to life deep within her and she stepped back deliberately from the pool's edge.

Rocco said hesitantly, 'Gracie…?'

And then she ran and dived right in, barely breaking the surface, the flash of intense colour in her dress gliding away under the surface to the other end.

CHAPTER NINE

Rocco stared after Gracie, shocked. The irritation and anger he'd felt sparking when she'd tried to articulate what was between them was fading. Something else was blooming inside him, along with remorse for lashing out just now. It was a feeling of euphoria. The kind of euphoria he'd felt only once before, when he'd seen horror and disbelief dawn in his father's eyes at knowing that his worthless bastard son had surpassed even his own phenomenal wealth.

Gracie's head broke the surface of the water at the other end of the pool at that moment. Her dress, magnified under the water in a cascade of different colours, rippled out around her body. She looked impossibly wild and free, like a sea nymph, her hair slicked back in a stain of dark red.

Rocco felt the first fat drops of monsoon rain fall as he bent and pulled off his shoes and socks.

He dived in expertly, crossing the length of the pool in half the time it had taken Gracie. He saw those slim pale legs, the dress billowing around them, and reached for her underwater and pulled her down. Her eyes were wide when Rocco pressed his mouth to hers.

When they broke the surface of the water together, a few long seconds later, Gracie tore her mouth away and sucked in deep breaths. The rain was torrential now, and she tipped back her head and laughed out loud. Her arms were tight around Rocco's neck and his hands were on her waist.

She looked at him, giddy from the shock of diving into the pool and then seeing him do the same. 'The rain *is* warm!'

'Why do you believe nothing I say?' he growled, and kissed her again.

Gracie pushed away the dart of hurt at the thought it was more apt for her to say that to him, and gave up and lost herself in the kiss. She didn't want to think about what had just passed between them moments before. She didn't want to think about what it meant to lose control like this with Rocco. She just wanted to give herself up to it.

When Rocco backed her against the wall of the pool and started to peel down the stretchy material of the dress she trembled with anticipation. Even though the rain was as warm as the pool, goosebumps came up on her skin.

He pulled her dress down her arms and all the way to her waist, so that her breasts were bared, nipples tight. As he bent his head to pay homage to those peaks Gracie had to breathe in deep at the sight of Rocco, in a shirt which was now completely see-through and plastered to his strong back. His dark skin shone through in patches. Hair slicked back against his skull.

His mouth was relentless. Gracie leant back against the wall, the rain coming down into her face. The sensuality of the weather and the moment was intoxicating. The sounds of the busy city drifted up from the streets far, far below. Gracie put her arms out along the wall of the pool and arched into Rocco even more. She felt him yank the dress down over her hips and off. She could see it drift off along the floor of the pool like a puddle of bright colours.

His hand was in her panties now, his palm putting pressure on her clitoris, and one long finger delved through her secret folds, seeking where her body was already clenching in anticipation. Gracie's lower body thrust against him, silently urging him on as she lifted her hands to reach for his shirt, ripping it open in her haste. He released his hand and arms to let her yank it off, and then he pulled her panties down her legs.

Gracie was now completely naked, while Rocco still wore his trousers. His hand was between her legs again and his mouth on her breast. Warm rain drenched them, and the pool water lapped around them with increasing intensity.

'Rocco,' she said brokenly, when he slid two fingers inside her, stroking back and forth. 'I need more. I need you.'

He pulled his head back, fingers stilling. Eyes dazed, cheeks flushed. His fingers were deep inside Gracie, he could feel the wet clamp of her body, and his own ache became urgent. With a swift move he'd lifted her out of the pool to sit on the ledge. Then he pulled himself out with the minimum of effort.

He gently lifted her up into his arms and laid her down on a nearby sunbed. Pressing a swift kiss to her mouth, he muttered something about protection and disappeared for a second, only to return just as swiftly. Gracie took in the stark planes of his face. The glitter in his eyes. He put the foil-wrapped protection between his teeth for a moment as he jerkily yanked off of his soaked trousers and briefs. Ripping open the package, he smoothed the sheath onto his erection and came back to Gracie.

She felt as if she'd become one with the elements. Rocco came between her legs and said gutturally, 'I want to taste you so badly, but I need this more…'

'What do you—? *Ohhhh*…' Gracie moaned when she

felt him thrust into her. She gave up all attempts to speak or think and wrapped her legs around his waist, locking her feet behind him, urging him deeper and deeper, until they both splintered apart under the stormy clouds and driving rain.

They lay for a long time like that, with Rocco still deep within her. Little aftershocks made her tremble uncontrollably every few seconds. Eventually Rocco moved, coming up on his arms. He disengaged himself and Gracie winced slightly because she was sensitive.

He pressed a kiss to her mouth. 'I hurt you...'

She shook her head. 'No. You didn't hurt me.' Her conscience pricked at that—perhaps not physically but emotionally...she didn't want to go there.

Rocco got up and disappeared for a moment, and then came back. He held out a fluffy robe for Gracie, who took it gratefully and sat up to put it on. Rocco had tied a towel around his waist and looked down at her.

'I'm going to take a shower, join me?'

Gracie shook her head even as her traitorous mind was screaming *yes!* She needed space for a moment. 'I think I might sit out here for a bit.'

He shrugged. 'As you wish,' he said, and went inside. Gracie couldn't stop her eyes greedily devouring his lean form as he went. When he'd disappeared she sighed and pulled the robe tight around her, drawing her knees up to her chest, wrapping her arms around herself. The rain had stopped and the clouds had moved off. Stars were twinkling again. The humid air was sucking up all the excess moisture. It was as if the storm had materialised just to accompany that mad passion, and now that it was over the storm was too.

She saw the detritus of what had just happened around them. The colourful shimmer of her dress at the bottom of the pool. Her coral-coloured panties floating on the surface of the water along with Rocco's shirt. His trousers and briefs strewn on the ground. She groaned and dropped her head to her knees. One minute she'd been standing there, telling him she didn't normally do this, and within seconds she'd been ripping his shirt off like a woman possessed.

He was right. It was *insane*. She didn't doubt that with his other women—his usual women—he was a lot more civilised and restrained. None of this messy passion.

No wonder he resented it.

She'd seen the look on his face just before he'd jumped into the pool, as if he were battling with something inside himself.

Gracie felt a yearning welling up inside her. She didn't want Rocco to resent this—or *her*. She wanted a chance to make him change his mind about her properly, not just this tenuous sliver of trust that could break at any moment. She wanted to persuade him that she and her brother *weren't* just some opportunists who came from a dubious background.

She heard a noise and looked up to see him re-emerging from the suite. He had a fresh towel wrapped around his waist and was rubbing at his hair with another towel. Gracie felt exposed all over again, as if he might read that awful yearning on her face.

Brightly she asked, 'Nice shower?'

He nodded, and then smiled wickedly. 'Would have been nicer with you in it.'

He came and sat down on the lounger next to hers and his clean scent washed over her, making her belly tighten with a shaft of need. Inexplicably Gracie felt dirty all of a sudden, when she recalled their explosion of passion.

She glanced away, feeling prickly. 'I like it out here.'

His voice was wry. 'You can't stay out here all night.'

She shrugged minutely. 'To be honest, the suite…the hotel…it's all a bit intimidating. I feel like I'm tainting it with my presence.'

Rocco went still. 'That's crazy…what are you talking about?'

She glanced at him. and then away again when she saw him frowning. 'It's like I'm not meant to be here. When I was about nine one of our foster parents took Steven and I to a stately home.' Gracie smiled and said self-consciously, 'She was one of the good ones… It was a grand old house. We had to get the train from London. It had these huge rooms—so beautiful, full of antiques and paintings. After a while I got lost. The group had gone on and I couldn't find them. I wandered into a room full of tiny porcelain dolls.'

Gracie grimaced a little, remembering.

'Obviously the people who owned the house had some kind of collection. I was fascinated, and picked one up to look at. Suddenly I felt a hand on my shoulder and I got such a fright I dropped it and it smashed on the ground. This woman was standing over me, shrieking about how I was a common little thief and to get out.' She shivered at the memory. 'I was so terrified I ran and ran, and finally found the group. I kept expecting to feel that hand on my shoulder again.'

Gracie felt embarrassed. Why on earth had she even started telling this story? But Rocco just looked at her, his face obscured in the dark.

She shrugged again, properly embarrassed now. 'Earlier, when we came in, and at the function too, I felt as if a hand was going to land on my shoulder at any moment and someone would ask how I'd got in.'

A little roughly, Rocco said, 'You have as much a right to be in these places as anyone else.'

Gracie half smiled. 'Well, I don't really. But it's nice of you to say.'

Rocco stood up then, with a hand outstretched, as if to leave and take her with him. Gracie stood up too, about to take his hand, but then she stopped. His closed-off expression made something rise up within her—a desperate need for him to understand, and *see*.

'Wait. I want to tell you something else.'

He dropped his hand, his jaw clenched. 'Gracie, you don't need to tell me these stories.'

His clear reluctance galvanised her. 'They're not *stories*—and, yes, I do need to tell you.' She continued before he could protest. 'Steven…my brother…we're twins.' Her mouth twisted. 'Non-identical obviously. I'm older by twenty minutes—he nearly died when he was born. When we were small he was puny and had big thick glasses. I got used to protecting him from bullies. He was never able to deal with things like I could. He never got over our mother leaving us…'

Gracie's voice shook with passion.

'He was too smart, too quiet. He was always a natural target. It might be hard to believe because of his actions, but he never wanted that life…to be in a gang, to get involved with drugs.'

'So why did he, then?' Rocco almost sneered.

Gracie flinched minutely but stood tall. Emotion constricted her voice. 'They beat him down—literally. One day he got so badly beaten that he almost ended up in hospital. They broke him. It was easier to go along with what they wanted than to fight it. Even though I did my best to stop him. We were only fourteen. They had him hooked on alcohol within months. Drugs came soon after. He dropped out of school. Gave up.'

'And yet you defend him even now?'

Again Rocco had that slightly sneering tone. Gracie looked at him, feeling a little disembodied. How could she even begin to explain the rich tapestry that bound her and her brother together?

She nodded slowly. 'Yes, I defend him—and I would defend him for ever. Just like he defended me.'

Rocco frowned, impatience palpable in his lean form. 'What do you mean? Defended you from what?'

Gracie knew her words were going nowhere, but she couldn't stop now. 'There was one foster home—it was miraculous, really, that we got to stay together all the time.' She took a deep breath. 'There was a man in this home. He used to look at me, and touch me when no one was around. Nothing serious at first—just a pat on the bottom or a pinch on my arm. But then one night he came into my room when his wife was away.'

Gracie could feel bile rising and forced it down.

'He sat on my bed and started telling me what he wanted to do with me. Steven was in the room next to mine with another boy. I was on my own. I was so scared I couldn't move or speak. Just when the man was about to get into bed beside me Steven came in. He didn't say anything. He just waited for the man to get up and leave, and from that night until we left that house he slept in my bed, even as his own life was falling apart. He never left me alone. Not once.'

Rocco looked at Gracie's pale face. Her words were like atom bombs detonating in his head and body. He wanted to rant and rage—throw the terrace furniture out over the balcony. He wanted to hug Gracie close and never let her go ever again. He trembled with it. Emotion was thick and acrid, gripping him by the throat. To think of that man touching her. And to think of her brother and what he'd been through. That he'd been beaten viciously enough to give in to that awful wasted life. Even now Rocco could see her brother's face, clear and burning with eagerness in his office, impressing him with his zeal because it had reminded him of his own hunger to succeed.

And yet her brother had still turned around and made a fool of Rocco's gut instinct, had betrayed him.

Rocco had been through the same trials…worse. And he hadn't given in—*never*. He clung to that assertion now, like a drowning man finding a piece of floating wood in a choppy ocean. He couldn't touch Gracie right now. If he did he felt as if the emotions seething in his gut would overwhelm him completely and throw him straight back to where he'd come from, what he'd left behind all those years before.

With a huge effort Rocco thrust down the thick, cloying emotion and stepped back from Gracie and those huge eyes.

He heard the words coming out but wasn't really aware of them. 'This changes nothing. All evidence points to the fact that he *hasn't* changed one bit. Don't try my patience telling me these things.'

Rocco turned and strode back into the suite, feeling as if his insides were splintering apart into a thousand pieces.

Gracie looked at Rocco walking away and felt numb with hurt and rejection. She realised now why she'd told him more than she'd ever told anyone else. Not even Steven had ever mentioned out loud what had almost happened that night so long ago. It had been too horrific to contemplate. Yet Gracie had just told Rocco as if it had cost her nothing. But it was costing her dearly. Because she knew now what lay beneath this self-destructive desire to expose herself to him no matter what the consequences.

She was falling in love with him.

* * *

Rocco wasn't surprised when he was still tossing and turning an hour later. What he wasn't prepared for was the ache in his gut and the way the vast emptiness of the bed beside him was affecting him. He drew back the covers and sat up, his parting words to Gracie ringing in his head. He cursed her. But even as he did he cursed himself more.

All he could see in his mind's eye now was that picture of Gracie and Steven when they'd been small. Her brother's scared-looking little face with those huge glasses and Gracie looking so strong beside him. Like a little warrior. He found himself feeling *jealous*—of her brother. That she cared so much for him. That they had such a bond.

It had been easier to hurl those words at her and walk away than deal with the emotion. It opened up far too many chasms. And yet he couldn't go on like this. He felt as if he was missing a limb.

Rocco went outside to the patio. He could see her curled up shape on a sun lounger in the dim moonlight and he felt the ache in his chest intensify into a physical pain. *Damn her.* He walked over and saw that their clothes were neatly folded and piled up. Her dress was a damp stain of colour against the ground. He looked at her, steeling himself for the inevitable effect.

Her face was relaxed, her hair rippling around her, looking very red against the pale cream lounger. Legs drawn up in that foetal pose she liked. His gut clenched when he thought of how her brother had protected her, and Rocco realised that he was jealous even of that.

He fought the urge to turn and walk away again. He bent down and scooped her up into his arms. She woke up and braced herself against him, resisting him.

'Wait…' Her voice sounded sleepy and sexy.

Rocco was already responding. He gritted his jaw and

said, 'Enough. You've made your point and I've made mine.'

He set her back and looked into those huge eyes, and felt that falling sensation again.

'I didn't mean to be so sharp.' He shook his head and forced the tender feeling from his belly. 'You don't have to tell me anything, Gracie. It doesn't change the situation we're in regarding your brother.'

Her hands were on his chest. Her voice was husky with emotion. 'You mean you don't want me to tell you anything because you're not interested?'

Rocco felt that tenderness inching back, together with a need to reassure her, and crushed it, feeling more ruthless than he'd ever been in his life. He concentrated on remaining immune to Gracie's appeal.

'Why your brother has done what he has is irrelevant to me. I deal in concrete things and he stole money from me. *You*, however, are far more relevant right now, and I don't want to talk about your brother or your past any more. Deal?'

Gracie was wide awake now, and could feel Rocco's intensity reaching out and sucking her in. He desperately wanted her to say yes. She could feel it. Even now, in spite of the hurt and rejection, she could fool herself into thinking she saw something deep in his eyes. Something vulnerable and exposed. She wanted this man with a hunger that shamed her. Even as she desperately wanted to be able to reject him, to inflict pain on him the way he'd done to her. But she couldn't.

Hating herself, and the feeling of inevitability that washed through her, she said with a small voice, 'Deal.'

To her relief Rocco didn't grin with triumph, or—look mildly pleased with her capitualtion. He just looked intense and serious as he picked her up in his arms and took her back into the bedroom.

Landing in New York two days later was a different experience from landing in Bangkok. Far below them was a sea of grey buildings as far as her eye could see, vastly different from the lush green paddy fields.

Rocco was working across the aisle from her, a frown between his eyes as he studied papers.

She looked back to the view. Since the other night it had been as if a proper truce existed between them. They were careful to talk only about neutral topics. Rocco had even taken time off from his meetings to take Gracie to Bangkok's stunning Grand Palace, and she'd wandered around in complete awe at the designs of the buildings with their vast marble terraces.

The style of the palace was eclectic: soaring Palladian arches and columns mixed with traditionally ornate Thai roofs. There was an entire temple devoted to a tiny Emerald Buddha which was placed high on an altar above the crowd. There was also a large model of the Cambodian temple of Angkor Wat, one of the places that had always fascinated Gracie.

She'd spent long minutes going round and round it, and had looked up to find Rocco leaning on a nearby wall just staring at her. She still felt weak inside when she thought of that look.

He'd woken her very early the previous morning and had led her, grumbling and sleepy, outside the hotel. She'd only noticed then that he was casually dressed in shorts and T-shirt. To her delighted surprise there had been a Tuk-Tuk waiting to take them to one of the floating markets, where they'd got into a boat and seen Buddhist monks in their distinctive orange robes accepting alms from the locals.

Gracie had been deeply moved by Rocco surprising her like that with a dawn visit to the markets before the hordes of tourists arrived, and the ride back through the city with the kamikaze Tuk-Tuk driver had been exhilarating.

'What are you thinking about?'

Gracie jumped and looked at Rocco, and her heart turned over. She'd refused to let her mind go back to her revelation that she was falling for him. Far too dangerous. If she didn't think about it, she thought weakly, perhaps the feeling would go away.

She forced a smile now, and said lightly, 'I was just thinking that the last woman you took to Bangkok probably didn't enjoy the Tuk-Tuk ride half as much as I did.'

Rocco said nothing for a moment, and he sounded almost surprised when he admitted, 'I've never taken anyone to Bangkok with me before.'

Gracie's heart swelled dangerously in her chest. As if to counteract it she said lightly, 'I'm sure you've brought them to New York, though.'

Rocco looked straight at her, as if sending her a warning. She was straying into dangerous territory. Very clearly he said, 'Yes, of course I've brought women to New York. I'm here much more frequently.'

Rocco looked away from Gracie and back to his papers. He'd been pretending for nigh on an hour now to be engrossed in work, when all he'd been aware of was each minute movement she made. He almost laughed out loud at the notion that any of his previous lovers would have got into a motorised rickshaw even if he'd paid them to do it. But Gracie had loved it as it had swerved and barrelled through the chaotic Bangkok traffic. And he'd loved it too. He couldn't remember the last time he'd just taken time off to look at the sights. To enjoy a place. *Never*, came back the succinct answer.

Going into the Grand Palace, the staff had been strict about the dress code. Gracie had been wearing a vest top over shorts. The staff had a facility to make sure everyone was dressed appropriately, so she had had to put on a huge billowing plaid shirt and skirt to cover up her arms, shoulders and bare legs.

He'd braced himself for a fit of feminine pique, but she'd just been worried that she'd offended the staff and then, when assured that she hadn't, she'd giggled at how ridiculous she must look. She hadn't looked ridiculous at all. He'd ached to pull her behind the sacred *wats* and do very unsacred things with her.

Rocco welcomed the skyline of New York coming closer and closer. In this city he would feel safer around Gracie, and he would keep her at a distance if it killed him. Bangkok had been a mistake. It had been way too raw.

Just thinking of that made him picture Gracie jumping into the pool in that dress, and with a barely stifled curse Rocco forced himself to concentrate until the page he was looking at blurred.

Gracie was very aware as they drove into the city of Rocco being distant. He was more businesslike than she'd ever seen him. She refused to let his mood upset her and stared in awe at the famously iconic skyline of New York as they crossed one of the many bridges into Manhattan. As they drove onto the island and the buildings soared up around them she saw all the yellow taxis and was enraptured.

Famous designer names glittered at her on Fifth Avenue, and then the green trees of Central Park materialised. With the park to their right, the car pulled up outside an Art Deco style building with a huge awning over the pavement.

Gracie was helped out of the car by a smiling doorman in a uniform and the summer heat hit her. It was totally different from the heat in Thailand, but just as intense—even in the morning.

The doorman was greeting Rocco. 'Welcome back, Mr de Marco, it's been too long!'

They walked through a cool lobby to where the concierge was waiting with the lift doors open. They stepped in and the lift smoothly ascended and came to a halt. The doors opened straight into a private corridor and the penthouse apartment. Gracie thought she'd seen pretty much everything by now, but this was palatial and stupendous on a whole new level. Everything was cream and gold. Carpets so thick you literally sank into them. Abstract oil paintings on the walls showed Rocco's taste for mixing the old with the new again. Antiques perched on small, elaborately designed tables. Huge cream couches were piled high with cushions.

Rocco was opening French doors on the other side of the room and Gracie followed dumbly, nearly too afraid to breathe. She stepped out into the morning air to see a vast terrace stretching what looked like the length of the building, with potted trees and artfully tamed flower boxes.

Rocco was standing with his hands on his hips, watching her, and Gracie joked weakly, 'Where's the pool?'

Rocco gestured with his head. 'Downstairs in the gym on the lower level.'

'Oh.'

'It's nice,' he said redundantly. 'It has a view out onto the park.'

Gracie felt seriously overwhelmed. She walked over to the wall and looked out to see one of the most famous city parks in the world stretching away either side of her. People walked along the streets below and looked like ants.

She could see a big open green space in the middle of the park. And a lake.

Again Gracie joked. 'I'm surprised you're not in the highest skyscraper so you can see the furthest.'

She wasn't looking at him, so she didn't see how his jaw clenched. And then he replied easily, 'Ah, yes, but the Upper East Side is the best address.'

Gracie looked around at Rocco to see him glance at his watch and say, 'Look, I have to head out now. I've got back-to-back meetings all day.'

For once she was glad at the prospect of a bit of space. She nodded her head. 'Okay. I'll just…settle in…'

Rocco took something out of his wallet and handed it to her. 'Here—take this. Why don't you go shopping?'

Gracie took the black credit card automatically and looked at it. She was barely aware of Rocco peeling something else from the wallet and putting it down on the table saying, 'You'll need some cash too, for taxis. I'll have Ruben downstairs give you a map and some directions. We've got a function to go to this evening, so I'll see you back here at six…okay?'

Gracie looked at Rocco and sensed his impatience to be gone. She just nodded again, feeling a little numb. 'Fine. See you later.'

There was a moment when it looked as if he wanted to say something, but then he turned and walked out of the apartment. A few seconds later a woman appeared, wiping her hands on an apron, and introduced herself as Consuela, Mr de Marco's housekeeper.

Gracie shook her hand. The woman was clearly a huge fan of Rocco. She insisted on showing Gracie around all four *en suite* bedrooms, two dining rooms, one informal sitting room, one formal drawing room, the gym and pool, sauna room, a massive kitchen and two further bathrooms.

When her head was spinning she let Consuela get back to work and set about unpacking her things and deciding what she would do for the day. She was determined to try and not think about Rocco for at least five whole minutes. And she resolved to find an internet café and see if there was an e-mail from Steven.

At lunchtime Rocco came back to the apartment. He cursed himself for his weakness, and wasn't prepared when Consuela informed him that Gracie had gone out a couple of hours before.

He went into the bedroom but there was no note—just their bags, which had been unpacked. He cursed. Why *would* she have left a note?

He was on his way back out, feeling thoroughly disgruntled, when he noticed something on the chest of drawers. It was his credit card and the few notes he'd left for Gracie, less only about twenty dollars. As if she'd literally taken just enough to get her downtown.

Rocco laughed at himself harshly. Had he *really* expected she would head straight for the designer boutiques on Fifth Avenue? This was the woman who had personally taken the diamond necklace and earrings back to the shop in the hotel in Bangkok.

Feeling even more disgruntled now, Rocco scooped up the card and left the cash, cursing himself for even coming to check up on her and trying to ignore the tight feeling when he imagined her finding her way around or seeing the sights on her own.

It was only when he was in his car and heading back downtown that his insides went cold and he realised that he'd effectively let Gracie go. Now and in Bangkok he'd left her to her own devices, and at any moment—like *right now*—she could be disappearing into thin air.

The fact that he'd trusted her so implicitly made him extremely nervous, and to his absolute chagrin he couldn't concentrate on one thing for the rest of the afternoon until he'd got confirmation from the concierge that she'd returned to the apartment. He did not relish the relief that made him feel so weak.

CHAPTER TEN

W<small>HEN</small> Gracie returned late that afternoon she was exhausted but happy. Well—she made a face at her sweaty reflection in the mirror over the hall table as she put down her bag—she wasn't *happy,* exactly. She'd have been happy if she'd had Rocco with her to share the delights of climbing to the top of the Empire State Building, and she'd have been happier if she hadn't had to sit in Central Park on her own eating a sandwich.

She worried her lower lip with her teeth. And she'd have been happy if there had been an e-mail from Steven, but there had been nothing waiting for her in her mailbox when she'd found an internet café. She'd sent an e-mail to his address anyway, in the futile hope that she might hear something back.

Sighing now, she went outside to take in the majestic view of Central Park again.

She'd had to realise as she had gone around on her own that Rocco hadn't brought her on this trip to hold her hand and be her guide—no matter how nice and thoughtful he'd been in Bangkok. The sooner she remembered that the better.

Leaning on the wall overlooking Central Park, Gracie smiled to herself, feeling a little bemused. Was this how it was for Rocco normally? He'd give his credit card to his current mistress, she'd shop all day and then flaunt herself like a peacock on his arm in the evening?

'You didn't take the credit card.'

Gracie whirled around with a squeal, her heart hammering at the sight of Rocco lounging nonchalantly against the terrace door. It was as if she'd conjured him up. 'You scared me. I didn't hear you come in.'

Rocco came towards Gracie. Something in his eyes looked dangerous and she backed against the wall.

She gulped. 'No, I didn't take the card. Why would I? I don't need anything. You bought me enough clothes to last a dozen trips abroad.'

Rocco's face was hard. He enclosed Gracie by putting his hands on the wall behind her. She fought not to let his unique scent and presence weaken her.

He sounded irritated. 'You don't get it, do you? That's what you're *meant* to do. So tell me what you *did* do, then.'

Fire rose within her and Gracie matched his harsh tone. 'For your information I *borrowed* twenty dollars and went downtown, where I took some money out of a hole in the wall from my own account. Then I queued for two hours and went to the top of the Empire State Building. After that I walked all the way back to the park and bought a sandwich and ate it. Is that all right?' Gracie felt guilty for not mentioning the internet café, but Rocco seemed too volatile for her to bring Steven into the mix.

'No, damn you, it's not all right.'

Rocco's head descended and his hands closed around her arms. His kiss was harsh and demanding. Gracie tried to refuse to let him do this—take out his anger on her because she wasn't like his other women—but he was relentless, and she couldn't resist. So she fought fire with fire.

Fingers digging deep into his hair, her whole body arched towards him, hips grinding into his. At least *this* was honest between them. This transcended all thought and rationale and reduced them to base desires that had to be sated or they would die.

Their fragile truce had just been smashed.

He picked her up in his arms and Gracie couldn't help pressing kisses all over his jaw and neck. She was already opening his shirt and undoing his tie. When they got to the bedroom Rocco lowered her down onto the bed and stripped off his jacket and tie, ripping open his shirt. Gracie pulled her top over her head and yanked down the shorts she'd been wearing, kicking off her sandals.

When Rocco was gloriously naked he came down beside her and Gracie just looked at him, unable to stop her heart from swelling or from touching his stubbled jaw with one hand. She couldn't hold it back. 'I missed you today,' she whispered.

Rocco just looked at her, and something flashed in his eyes before they darkened. 'Don't say that. I don't want to hear it.'

'Well, tough,' Gracie said obstinately. 'Because I did miss you and I've just said it again.'

With a growl Rocco came over her and silenced her with his mouth, his hands roving over her body, removing her bra and panties until she was as naked as he. And then she couldn't even have articulated her name as Rocco took her with a thoroughness that had her crying out over and over again.

'And who is your companion?'

Gracie smiled tightly at the anaemic-looking woman with hair so set in a ball around her head that she feared it would go up in flames if she stood too close to a light. She could have been anywhere from forty to sixty-five, her face was so immobile and smooth.

'Gracie O'Brien,' Rocco was murmuring beside her.

The woman sent a disparaging look up and down, taking in Gracie's sparkling black floor-length dress.

'Ah, yes. Well, I might have imagined you're Irish, with the red hair and pale skin.'

Gracie smiled sweetly. 'Actually my mother was English, and I was born and grew up there, but, yes, my father was Irish.'

The woman's brows arched. 'I see.' And then, as if thoroughly bored by Gracie, and also not happy that she'd even spoken, she turned to Rocco and linked her arm with his. 'Now, Rocco darling, tell me all about Bangkok. I'm dying to hear about your deal with the Larrimar Corporation.'

The woman was expertly manoeuvreing Rocco away from Gracie, but he stalled in his tracks, forcing the woman to stop too. He smiled at her, but Gracie shivered. She'd seen that smile many a time, and was glad it wasn't directed at her for once.

He extricated his arm from the woman's claw-like clutch and took Gracie's hand, pulling her firmly to his side, saying nothing but making it very clear that she was not to be ignored. Gracie tried to ignore the jump her heart gave, and watched with amusement as the woman constantly tried to force Gracie out—only to have Rocco pull her even more firmly into his side.

Gracie tuned the conversation out. People-watching was too fascinating. They were in a function room in an exclusive hotel on the other side of Central Park from Rocco's apartment. They'd just eaten a sumptuous dinner at a huge banquet table with about two hundred guests, and had now moved into another exquisite room which led to an emormous terrace lit with hundreds of candles.

Gracie saw people milling around outside and suddenly wanted to breathe some fresh air. She tried to break free from Rocco, but his grip was like iron. She had to elbow him in the ribs before he looked down.

She smiled sweetly at the snobbish woman and said to Rocco, 'I'm just going to get some air.'

Rocco had to battle a huge reluctance to let Gracie go but finally he did. He watched her walk away through the crowd, her red hair like a glowing beacon, making people stop and turn around to look at her. She was so vibrant and alive compared to most people in the room. How had he only really noticed that now? And yet wasn't that what had caught him the very first time he'd seen her?

When they'd been driven the short distance in the car from his apartment to the hotel earlier, Gracie had said to Rocco wistfully, 'We could have walked through the park.'

Rocco had looked at her and shook his head. 'No, Gracie, we couldn't.'

She'd stuck her tongue out and said, 'Spoilsport,' and he'd remembered what she'd said earlier, about missing him, and he had all but fallen out of the car in his haste to get away. And yet just now he hadn't been able to let her go.

'She's different.'

Rocco swung back. He was afraid he'd spoken out loud. 'I'm sorry?'

Helena Thackerey was an inveterate snob, but she was also very shrewd and a tough financial negotiator.

'I said, she's *different*.'

Rocco schooled his features, defensive hackles rising. 'Yes, she is. But there's nothing more to our relationship than any other I've had.'

The older woman snorted and looked a lot more human for a moment. 'Tell that to someone who might believe you, de Marco.' She leant forward and said, *sotto voce*,

'I like her. She's got spunk. Not like those asinine up-percrust bores you usually date.'

Gracie ploughed her way through the crowd, oblivious to some of the wealthiest people in Manhattan, and made it out to the terrace. She grabbed some water from a passing waiter and stood taking in the magical view of New York at night. She stretched out over the wall to try and see as far as she could.

A voice came from right behind her and sent a shiver through her. 'That's Harlem up to your left.'

Rocco stepped even closer, so her back and buttocks were flush against his front, and she could feel him hardening against her. She leaned her head back against his chest and said breathily, 'You're insatiable.'

He put an arm around her middle and pressed even closer. She heard a throaty, 'Let's get out of here. I've had enough of New York's finest for one evening.'

Gracie turned in his arms and looked up. She rolled her eyes and said, 'Me too, and I'm *so* over these views of Central Park.'

Rocco bit back a laugh and bent his head. Gracie hated the way she loved how she could make him laugh.

He said, close to her ear, 'That's a pity, because when we get back I want to recreate this exact position—except I want your dress gone and your legs around my waist.'

Gracie gulped and put her glass down on a table as Rocco unceremoniously hauled her from the room.

Back in Rocco's apartment, Rocco advanced towards Gracie, who was standing obediently at the wall overlooking Central Park—from the other side now. She shivered with anticipation just watching him take off his jacket and bow tie, opening his shirt. He came close and the air vibrated between them, and then he took her by surprise and kissed her so sweetly on the mouth that she put her hands to his chest.

When he broke away and just looked at her Gracie suddenly wanted more than just the physical. Softly she asked, 'How can you stand socialising with people like that all the time?'

Rocco went still. 'What do you mean?'

'Well…like that woman. She was so rude.' Gracie flushed. 'And Honora Winthrop was rude.'

Rocco took Gracie's hands and pulled them down. He stepped to her side and rested his hands on the wall. Subtle tension radiated out from his body.

'Helena is not too bad, actually. A lot of her manner is bluster. She was one of the few people who helped me when I first came to New York as a green negotiator.'

Gracie frowned. She couldn't imagine Rocco ever not being completely experienced and in control.

He slid her a glance. 'She liked you. She said you've got spunk.'

Gracie smiled tentatively. 'Okay, so maybe I was wrong about her. But I wasn't wrong about Honora.'

Rocco's face got serious. 'No. She's an out-and-out bitch.'

Gracie looked up at him. 'So I don't understand how you could have ever contemplated marrying her?'

Rocco said nothing for a long moment, because he was wondering how he could explain that he'd never intended to take a wife for romantic reasons. Then he gestured with an arm towards the dark park. 'For *this*. You have to be accepted into this world to be really successful, and the only way to achieve that for someone like me is to marry into it.'

Gracie went still inside. 'What do you mean, for someone like you? Don't you come from this world too?'

She turned around so she was facing Rocco. After a long moment he shook his head. He gestured down to the pavements far below. His voice was tight. 'That's where I'm from. Exactly like you.'

Something deep inside Gracie was slotting into place. She'd always suspected there was more to Rocco. 'What do you mean, exactly like me? You can't mean that you grew up—?'

He looked at her and his eyes were fierce. 'On the streets? Struggling to survive in a hostile environment? That's exactly what I mean.'

Rocco looked away again and cursed violently in Italian. Gracie realised in that moment that she'd rarely, if ever, heard him speak his native tongue.

After a long moment he said, 'I don't have to talk about this.'

Gracie took a metaphorical step into the dark. Feeling her way. 'Why not?' *I won't be around for much longer*, she wanted to add, but it hurt too much.

Rocco stared into the black space of the park as if it held answers she couldn't see, and then he started talking in a low, emotionless voice that told her a multitude of things. He told her how he had been born and had grown up in the worst slum in Italy, in one of the poorest cities. He told her of his mother, who had been a prostitute, but a high-class prostitute—which was how it came to be that his father was one of the city's wealthiest men.

'My mother spent every penny on feeding her escalating drug habit. She had targeted my father on purpose to secure a future for herself through me. She'd even been smart enough to get a swab from him, so that she could do a DNA test as soon as I was born and have proof of his paternity. But my father didn't want to know. He had two daughters and he was a megalomaniac. He didn't want a son appearing on the scene to threaten his rule. And he especially didn't want a son by a prostitute who came from the slums to sully his perfect respectable world and reputation.'

Gracie could see Rocco's hands tighten on the wall.

'You can't even begin to imagine what that world was like. The constant noise, the calls from block to block that were code for rival gangs—a murder, a drug-drop. All day and all night. They used me as a lookout for rival gangs.'

His mouth twisted.

'We didn't have a call for the police. They never came. They were as corrupt as we were. There was no social services for us. I hated the brute force of that life, the lack of intellect over chaos and destruction. My mother lurched from one passionate crisis to another. I craved a more ordered world—without that constant drama and uncertainty, the ever-present danger.'

Gracie could feel shivers of shock going through her body. 'What happened to your mother?'

Rocco went very still. 'I found her dead with a needle sticking out of her leg when I was seventeen.'

Gracie put a hand on his arm. Her voice was choked. 'Oh, Rocco….'

He shook her hand off and speared her with that black gaze. 'I'm not telling you this for sympathy. I don't need sympathy. I never have. She didn't love me. She was too in love with getting her next fix or a wealthy patron.'

Gracie swallowed the lump in her throat. 'I'm sorry.'

He looked away again, and Gracie cradled her hand against her belly.

'I confronted my father one day outside his city *palazzo*. I knew where he lived. My mother had pointed it out to me enough times. It was just after she'd died. When I confronted him he spat at me and pushed me down and stepped over me. My two half-sisters were with him and didn't even look my way, even though they'd heard me call him Father. I watched them step into a chauffeur-driven car. I watched how they could just walk away from the unsavoury truth. I envied them their ease and protection. I envied their wealth, which gave them that protection.'

He smiled then, and it made fear inch up Gracie's spine.

'My father obviously had a word with one of his *men*. As soon as the car pulled away I was dragged into a nearby lane and beaten so senseless that I ended up in hospital. It was an effective warning. I never attempted to see him again. I left Italy and I vowed that one day I would look into my father's eyes and know that I had earned my place in his world, despite his rejection.'

Gracie looked at the hard jaw and the bunched up shoulders. She saw the faint scar running from his temple to his jaw and the smaller scars. She could well imagine that meeting between father and son, and could almost feel sorry for his father. She longed to reach out and touch Rocco now, to soothe his pain. But he was like a wild animal. He was raw.

She remembered something and said, 'That scar…on your shoulder. It was a tattoo, wasn't it?'

Rocco nodded. 'It meant I belonged to a certain part of the slum.' His mouth twisted. 'A certain faction. I got it removed when I came to England.'

'That's why you never speak Italian. You hate any reminders.'

Rocco dropped his head between his shoulders and said, in a deceptively soft voice, 'Just go, Gracie…leave me alone.'

Gracie took a step back, hurt blooming out from her

heart all over her body. She was terrified she'd start crying. She ached to comfort him. She started to step away, but got to the door and looked back. She saw Rocco standing there, head down, and realised that he'd always been a lone figure. Fighting the world around him while simultaneously longing to be part of it.

Resolution fired her blood, and she kicked off her shoes and walked back over to him. She slipped under one of his arms and came up so that his body formed a cage around her.

She looked up, straight into Rocco's face and his dark eyes. 'No, I won't leave. Because I don't think you really do want to be alone.' She reached up and placed her small palm on his rigid jaw. Her eyes caressed his mouth. 'I want you, Rocco. So much.'

The tension was thick enough to touch, and then suddenly it snapped. Rocco issued a guttural, 'Damn you!' and hauled Gracie up into his body so tightly she thought her back might break, but she bit her lip. She would not say a word. She could sense the violence in him, the untamed wildness that needed release, and she wanted desperately to be there for him in the only way he would allow her to be.

Rocco demanded and Gracie gave—over and over again. His kisses were brutal and electrifying. Their clothes were shed as they moved through the apartment, ripped and torn from their bodies in desperate haste.

Afterwards, Gracie couldn't even remember how they'd got to the bedroom—only that what had happened there had shown her how restrained Rocco had become to tame the natural wildness in him. And the long-simmering anger. Her body ached all over, but pleasurably. She knew her pale skin would be bruised. Rocco had nipped her with his teeth, and she shivered now to think of how she'd wanted him to bite her harder. He'd taken her from behind, with her hands wrapped around the bedposts, and it had been the most erotic thing she'd ever felt. The heavy weight of his body on hers as he'd crushed her to the bed and thrust into her over and over again.

She lifted her head now and looked at him. The innate tension in his body told her that he wasn't asleep. 'Rocco...?'

To her surprise he put an arm over his face and wouldn't look at her. She tried to pull it down and he said roughly, 'I can't look at you. I...I took you like an animal.'

Gently but firmly Gracie pulled his arm down and then moved over Rocco's body so she was lying on his chest with her legs either side of his hips. She put her hands to his face.

'Rocco de Marco. *Look* at me.' He opened his eyes, and she could have wept at the shame she saw. She swallowed back her own emotion. 'I am fine. I liked it.'

She pressed kisses to his jaw and mouth and down his neck. He put his hands around her upper arms and forcibly moved her back, coming up so that she had to lie on her back again.

'No. I can't do this.'

His expression was unreadable in the gloom. Gracie's heart stuttered as she watched Rocco get out of the bed, his tall, naked form magnificent in the dim light.

He said, without looking her way, 'Get some sleep, Gracie. We leave tomorrow at lunchtime.'

It was the hardest thing Rocco had ever done, to walk away from Gracie in that bed. He headed straight for the pool and dived in. He'd been aching to plunge into her body all over again as she'd straddled him. *'I am fine. I liked it.'* Her fervent words had scored his insides like a serrated knife.

She'd seen too much. Got too close. He'd never told about his past. He'd been so careful not to. Yet with the smallest amount of encouragement he'd spilled it all out to Gracie. And she'd accepted it unconditionally. Embraced it.

He'd taken her brutally, and she'd welcomed him every step of the way—had encouraged him. And in the process he had assuaged his pain so that his intense anger had faded and been replaced with a kind of strange peace. Even the shame he'd felt initially was fading.

As Rocco powered up and down the pool he hoped that the physical numbness he craved would somehow numb the feelings inside him. Because these were new feelings, not dark and twisted like the old ones, and somehow they were far more frightening than anything else he'd ever known.

At lunchtime the following day Gracie still felt a little shattered. It was as if an earthquake had happened last night, and she wasn't sure where anything stood any more. She'd woken late, after tossing and turning once Rocco had walked out so suddenly, and Consuela had informed her that Rocco had gone to his office.

She heard a noise and looked up from the TV. She hadn't been able to concentrate on the rolling news channel. Rocco stood in the doorway, looking incredibly austere and stern. Her stomach fell. She didn't need to wonder how things stood after last night. It was written all over him: rejection.

Gracie told herself she shouldn't be surprised. She'd pushed Rocco too far. He'd never forgive her for making him spill his guts. He was too proud.

She stood up slowly and tried to match his cool reserve, even though she shook on the inside. 'I'm ready to go.'

Rocco held up a piece of paper in his hand. 'Do you want to explain this to me?'

Gracie frowned and glanced at the paper. 'What are you talking about?'

Rocco held it up and read aloud in flat tones. *"Steven, where are you? Are you okay? Please contact me, I have so much to tell you. I need to know you're all right. Please, just let me know where you are. Send me a number so I can call you. We need to talk—I can help you."*

Gracie blanched. 'How did you get that?'

Rocco's eyes were black, and he bit out, 'It's his work e-mail address. I have someone checking Steven's inbox around the clock.'

Gracie's belly cramped. She felt guilty even though she had no reason to. 'I didn't tell you yesterday because you seemed so angry when you came back to the apartment. But I would have told you that I'd tried to contact him.'

Rocco arched a brow in a way Gracie hadn't seen him do for days. She wanted to hit him.

'You had a whole evening to tell me. This e-mail reeks of collusion. You were trying to warn him to stay away, or to arrange a meeting somewhere.'

Gracie swallowed. She could see how, in a certain frame of mind, it might read like that. If you mistrusted the person who wrote it—which Rocco patently did. She straightened her back and tried to ignore the feeling of her heart aching.

'That's how it might read to you. It's not how I meant it. I meant exactly what I said—I'm worried about him and want to know where he is. When I said I could help him I meant just that—if he gives himself up I intend to help him through whatever repercussions emerge from his actions.'

Rocco lowered the paper and smiled harshly. 'So

noble—and such lies. I think you were going to tell him you'd inveigled your way into his boss's bed and fed him stories designed to gain sympathy. Perhaps you wanted to be sure to corroborate each other's stories before he came forward like some penitent?'

Inveigled your way into his boss's bed. Stories. The words dropped into Gracie's head like poison-tipped arrows. He thought she'd set out to seduce him? The idea was laughable. She thought of the private things she'd shared with him. The fact that he saw them now as mere *stories* to gain sympathy nearly made her double over with pain.

She shook her head. It whirled dizzily. 'That's ridiculous.'

'No,' Rocco said harshly. 'What's ridiculous is that I've seriously underestimated you for so long. You're a conniving thief, just like your brother, and the lengths you'll go to to protect him are truly unbelievable.'

Gracie was shaking in earnest now. 'Need I remind you that *you* seduced *me*?'

Rocco's face was drawn from granite, the lines harsh. It was as if he couldn't hear her. 'From the moment we met at that function in London you've been playing me. You and your brother. He messed up and you're cleaning up his mess.'

Gracie looked at him. A numbness was spreading through her body. Rocco was immovable. A million miles from the raw, emotional man of last night. She wanted to accuse him of lashing out at her because she'd gone too deep and too far and exposed him. But she'd already exposed herself enough. If she displayed the emotion she was feeling it would show him that she felt something for him, and right now she would rather die than let him see that.

So she drew inwards, deep inside, to the place she'd

always retreated to for years. Whenever things got really bad. When her mother had left, and later when her nan had handed them over to Social Services. When her first lover had stood there and called her a slut for giving him her virginity. And when Steven had been taken to jail and she'd been alone.

She drew into the place where Rocco's words couldn't touch her any more and said woodenly, 'You seem to have it all figured out. What more is there to say?'

She looked at him but didn't see him. She only saw pain and anger at her own folly for thinking for a second that last night meant anything. For thinking that any of this meant anything.

His voice was clipped, harsh. 'There's nothing more to say. It's time to go.'

The journey back to London was a blur. Gracie had slept in the bedroom on the plane alone, tortured by vivid dreams of looking for Steven only to find Rocco waiting around corners with a savage expression on his face.

As Rocco's car pulled up outside his building in the cool dark night Gracie acknowledged that the effort to keep up her icy control was fading fast, and was being replaced by a flat, empty ache all through her body. She resolutely ignored Rocco when he joined her to step into the building.

For a split second she looked longingly at the empty street, and then felt her arm taken in a harsh grip. 'Don't even think about it.'

Gracie wrenched her arm away and glared up at him, her fire returning. 'Don't touch me. I'm not going to leave my brother to your mercy now.'

They were silent in the lift going up to the apartment, but to Gracie's chagrin, with the dissipation of the icy control she'd wielded all day, emotion was creeping back, and she had to consciously stop herself from remembering Rocco's tangible pain the night before, and the awful picture he'd painted of his life in Italy. He didn't deserve her sympathy. Not for one second. Especially not now.

When they got to the apartment George was there to greet them. Gracie felt like running into his huge barrel chest and blubbing all over him, but she didn't.

He handed some newspapers to Rocco and said, in a serious voice, 'There's a picture of you and Gracie in the tabloids.'

Rocco came in behind Gracie and opened out the next day's paper. She crept closer, forgetting her ire for a moment at the sight of a huge picture of her and Rocco at the party in New York and a caption underneath: *'Who is de Marco's latest flame-haired mistress?'*

Gracie felt sick. Rocco closed the paper after a long moment and said, 'Now we'll see how protective your brother really is.'

Gracie looked at him stupidly, trying to figure out what he meant, and then it hit her. Her mouth opened. She was aware of pain, even more pain, lancing her insides. 'You...' she framed shakily, 'you accused me of seducing you, but *you* set the whole thing up...taking me away with you so that my brother might see pictures of us and come out of hiding.'

Rocco's face was unreadable. His mouth thinned. 'It'll be interesting to see if your bond is as strong as you say it is.'

Gracie looked up at Rocco and couldn't see an inkling of the man she'd thought she was falling for. He'd never looked so cold and ruthless. 'You're a bastard.'

He smiled then, and it was cruel. 'You're absolutely right. I am.'

CHAPTER ELEVEN

ROCCO watched as Gracie finally turned around and walked away jerkily. He heard her door close and the lock turn. He cursed and threw the paper down, and went straight to the drinks cabinet and poured himself a whisky. His hands were shaking. He'd had a red mist over his vision all day, ever since his PA had handed him the printout of the e-mail when he'd been leaving his office to go and pick Gracie up.

He'd almost ignored it, thinking it was something irrelevant, but had then read it. At first he'd seen only the surface message. It had looked innocuous enough. But then, as he'd re-read it, he'd seen more and more—until by the time he'd got back to the apartment, where Gracie had been waiting so patiently, the words of the e-mail had become a gnarled black symbol of his humiliation at her hands the previous night. Lead had surrounded his heart.

All he'd been able to think about was how excruciatingly exposed he felt. How stupid he'd been to trust her so blindly, convincing himself all along that she was innocent. When he'd thought of the burgeoning sense of peace that had settled over him after his exhaustive swim, and how in the cold light of that morning he hadn't regretted baring his soul to her, he'd wanted to punch something.

All that time she'd been trying to contact her brother

because she believed she had Rocco right in the palm of her hand. Rational thought had fled. There was no room for it in the state of paranoia that Rocco had been plunged into.

He'd said things to her that had made her pale and look sick and he'd felt nothing but numb. Even when she'd visibly retreated to somewhere he couldn't reach and kept him at that icy distance he'd welcomed it. It was only when he'd spotted her wistful look towards freedom outside his building just now that something had pierced his fierce control. It had been a primal reflex not to let her go. To keep her by his side at all costs.

And now Rocco had to face the fact that he'd reacted from a place of deep, deep pain. A pain that could only be afflicting him because an equally deep emotion was involved. And he also had to face the fact that either every one of his cynical beliefs would be proved right, or he'd just made the most spectacular mistake of his life.

The following afternoon Rocco was pacing in his office by the window. Work was far from his mind. Gracie hadn't emerged from her room, and she hadn't answered when he'd knocked on her door. Only her hoarse, *'Go away!'* had stopped him from breaking the door down. He'd just now rung up to Mrs Jones, who'd told him worriedly that she was still in her room.

He felt a curious prickling sensation on his neck and turned around to see a familiar figure walking towards his office. His heart sank like a stone. His employees had stopped to look too, because they knew what this meant. Rocco knew it meant something more, though—something infinitely more important than a million euros. His heart spasmed in his chest. As he watched Steven Murray walk into his office with a furious look on his face he knew it meant that he'd made the biggest mistake of his life.

The only thing that roused Gracie from her catatonic state was a familiar voice. She was dimly aware that it was evening outside. She heard it again.

'Gracie, come on. Open the door. It's me.'

She sat up. It couldn't be. She had to be dreaming. Feeling as if it really might be a dream, she finally moved her legs and got up and went to the door. She opened it, and saw her brother standing on the other side.

For a long moment she just looked at him stupidly, not believing her eyes, and then the emotion she'd been denying herself erupted into noisy sobs and she threw herself into his skinny arms. He grabbed her tight and stroked her back and shushed her.

Without knowing how they'd got there, Gracie found herself sitting on a couch, with Steven pushing a glass with amber liquid in it into her hand.

She sucked in a shuddery breath, her face and eyes felt swollen. 'I don't drink.'

Her brother insisted. 'You do now—go on; you need it.'

Gracie took a sip and grimaced when her insides seemed to burst into flame. She coughed a little. As the drink brought her back to life and she registered that it was really her brother sitting in front of her panic gripped her. She grabbed his hand. 'Wait. You can't be here—Rocco is just downstairs. If he finds you—'

She stopped talking when she felt her skin tingle and saw Steven look at something—or *someone*—over her head. She turned to see a pale-looking Rocco with his hands in his pockets.

'I know he's here. He came to see me first when he arrived.' Rocco smiled faintly but it looked strained.

Gracie was tense. She didn't understand Rocco's lack of anger, or her brother's lack of urgency. She tore her eyes from Rocco. 'Steven…what…?'

He smiled and looked tired. 'It's a long story. I've explained everything to Mr de Marco. I was blackmailed, Gracie, by some guys I knew in prison. They knew where I was working and they had some knowledge of fraud and inside trading. They threatened to expose me to Mr de Marco. I was terrified I'd lose the best thing that had ever happened to me… The whole thing escalated until they wanted too much money and I panicked and ran…'

Steven glanced at Rocco, and Gracie saw the respect in his face.

'Mr de Marco has promised not to prosecute if I can help him track these guys down.' He looked back to Gracie. 'Depending on how much money we can recover, I'll still owe a lot to Mr de Marco—but he's offered me a job to get me back on my feet so I can start paying him back. Gracie, I don't deserve this chance. But I'm not going to mess up again. I promise.'

Gracie couldn't believe what she was hearing. She was in shock. And then she heard Rocco say to Steven, 'Would you give us a moment, here? Mrs Jones will show you to a room.'

Steven nodded and pressed Gracie's hands. 'Are you okay?'

Gracie wanted to laugh hysterically. She'd never been less okay. But she nodded her head and watched her brother walk out of the room with his loping, slightly awkward gait.

Rocco walked into her field of vision and Gracie could only look up at him, willing down the tendrils of sensation and feelings that were too close to the surface. 'Why did you do this? Why are you giving him a chance? After everything—'

'Everything I said?' he finished for her, in a voice so harsh she flinched minutely. Rocco cursed in Italian. 'I'm sorry.' He turned away then, as if he couldn't bear for her to look at him, and said rawly, 'God, Gracie. I'm so sorry.'

He turned back after long seconds.

'I was an idiot—a stupid, blind fool. When I read your e-mail I twisted it so that I could believe the worst. Last night in New York you got too close, too deep. I'd never told anyone about myself before, and yet with you...it all came out. And you didn't turn away in horror or shock. You embraced it.'

He pulled over a chair to sit in front of her. His eyes burned.

'I didn't set up the newspaper story. You have to believe that. When I saw the picture it was the first time I thought it might flush Steven out. I hadn't even considered that possibility before. But I let you believe I had because I was so desperate to push you away.'

Rocco grimaced, and Gracie could see the wildness in his eyes—but this was a different wildness.

'I knew deep down that you were none of the things I accused you of yesterday. I seduced you because I couldn't *not*.' He shook his head, disgust with himself palpable. 'I lashed out because I've never trusted anyone in my life until you. And then when Steven turned up today and came straight to me, demanding to know what was going on between us, the sheer evidence of the lengths he'd go to to make sure you were okay humbled me. I had nothing left to hide behind.'

A tiny flicker of hope burst to flame in Gracie's heart, as if a magical thaw was starting.

Rocco said fervently, 'I should never have kept you here

in the first place, but the truth is that it always had more to do with how you made me feel rather than anything to do with your brother.'

The flame inside Gracie trembled. 'What are you saying?'

Rocco took her hand. Gracie willed down the immediate physical reaction.

'I can't stop you leaving if you want to. But I don't want you to leave. I want you to stay…for as long as you want.'

'For as long as *I* want?' Gracie asked faintly. The fragile flame inside her sputtered dangerously.

Rocco nodded. 'We have something, Gracie. Something powerful.'

Gracie pulled her hand free of Rocco's. What he meant was that they had *desire*. Physical attraction. And he wanted her to stay until it had burnt itself out.

Before she could say anything he was grimacing slightly and looking at his watch. 'Look, I've got to go to a meeting. I can't reschedule it. Think about what I've said. We'll talk when I get back…okay?'

He just looked at her, and Gracie felt numb.

He said, *'Please?'* and she realised that he wasn't going to move until she said something. Dumbly she nodded. She saw relief relax his features.

He didn't say anything else. Just stood up and walked out.

Gracie might have nodded to signify assent, but she knew what she had to do. She had to leave—to get away. Rocco wanted a brief relationship. He'd said nothing about love. And she couldn't deal with that—not knowing how she felt. Not knowing how deeply in love with him she was. He could never have hurt her so badly yesterday if she didn't love him.

She was just a temporary diversion. Rocco would

choose an ice princess to be his partner some day, and
Gracie wanted to hate him for that—but how could she
when she knew how badly he craved that ultimate acceptance? When she knew how hard he'd struggled to leave
his past behind so he could get it? Didn't he deserve it
after the tragedy and pain he'd endured? She of all people
couldn't deny him that.

Moving on autopilot, Gracie packed her paltry belong-
ings and penned two brief notes—one for Rocco and another for her brother. She couldn't even bear to see Steven
right now, terrified he'd convince her to stay. When she
went to the entrance of the apartment to leave a different
bodyguard was on duty to let her out and she was glad.
Seeing George might have shattered her brittle control
completely.

Two weeks later.

Gracie was struggling through the dense crowd and had
to hold the full tray of empty glasses practically over her
head to get through. Even as she cursed, and sweat rolled
down her back and between her breasts, she tried to stop
herself from griping. With this job she would be able to
afford to move out of the hostel in a few weeks and find
somewhere cheap to rent. And once she had somewhere
of her own she would put aside a few hours every day and
work on her idea for the children's book.

Gracie heaved a sigh of relief when she saw the kitchen
doors ahead. She went in and put the tray down, but was
immediately handed another full tray of champagne by
her boss, who said cheerily, 'They're a thirsty lot tonight.'

She stifled a weary sigh and went out again. If anything the crowd seemed even denser now, and she looked
at the vast, unmoving sea of men in black and women in

glittering finery and wondered how on earth she could get through.

Resolutely she started to say, *'Excuse me...'* and, *'Sorry...'* but she wasn't making much progress. Suddenly a frisson of energy went through the crowd, as if someone special had arrived, and people were whispering. People were bunching together now and craning their necks. She rolled her eyes and clung on to the tray. No doubt it was some celebrity.

Then she heard someone say, 'Oh, my God, he's getting up on a table.' And then, 'Is that really him...?'

Through the hush that had fallen in the room Gracie heard a familiar voice ringing out. 'Gracie O'Brien, I know you're in here somewhere. Where are you?'

Her heart stopped dead. It couldn't be. She was hallucinating.

The voice came again, with familiar impatience, 'Dammit, Gracie, where are you?'

Now she knew she couldn't be imagining things.

Tentatively she looked up, straining to see over taller heads, and her breath stopped in her throat when she saw Rocco way above the crowd, head swivelling back and forth, hands on hips as he stood right in the middle of one of the sumptuous buffet tables.

He turned in her direction and she ducked too late. She heard his growl of triumph and the sound of feet hitting the floor. She tried to turn and run but by now people had crowded behind her so she was truly trapped.

As if in slow motion the crowd in front of Gracie parted like the Red Sea and Rocco was revealed. Tall and dark and gorgeous. In a pale blue shirt and dark trousers. Hands on hips. Those dark eyes homing in on her like a laser. His jaw was stubbled and he looked wild. Her hands were shaking so badly now that the glasses wobbled precariously on her tray. Rocco strode forward and took the tray out of her hands, passed it to a stunned pot-bellied man who stood nearby.

Then he turned back to Gracie. She just stood there and asked, 'Why are you here, Rocco? I made it clear in my note that I'm not interested in an affair.'

His mouth tightened and his eyes flashed. 'Yes, your succinct one-line note: *"Dear Rocco, I'm sorry but I'm not interested in an affair. Goodbye. Gracie." Dio.* I wanted to wring your neck when I got that.'

The entire crowd around them was so silent you could have heard a pin drop, but Gracie could only see one man. Her body was already responding. She clenched her hands tight and kept her eyes up.

'I meant what I said. I'm not interested in an affair.'

Rocco took a step closer and Gracie moved back.

'Neither am I.'

Gracie shook her head. 'But…you only said that we had *something*.'

'We do.'

Gracie felt futile anger rise along with confusion. 'Rocco…*why* are you here? I want you to leave me alone. I'm not interested—'

He took a step closer again. 'Tell me what you *are* interested in.'

Horror filled Gracie and she lied desperately. 'I'm interested in nothing with you.'

He smiled. 'Liar.'

Immediately she exploded. 'I'm *not* a liar. I've never lied…'

Rocco's tone turned soothing. 'I know, *cara*…but I'm afraid that you are lying about this.'

To her horror and disgust Gracie could feel tears spring into her eyes, and vaguely saw a horrorstruck look cross

Rocco's face. He reached for her and pulled her into him. It was heaven and hell. She couldn't move in his tight embrace.

'Damn you, Rocco.' She spoke into his chest and then he pulled her back slightly.

His hands were around her jaw, caressing her face, catching her tears. He sounded tortured. 'Don't cry, *piccolina*...please. I don't want to make you cry. Just tell me—what *are* you interested in?'

Gracie opened her mouth. She wanted to lash out at the hurt he'd caused her, and the beautiful pain he'd brought into her life by making her fall in love with him, but she couldn't. She looked up into his dark, harsh face and could only see the man she loved.

In a quivery voice she said simply, 'I'm interested in *you*, Rocco de Marco. I'm interested in everything about you. What moves you, what you want, what makes you happy. I'm interested in making you happy. I'm in love with you, and I'm interested in spending the rest of my life with you—not just having a brief fling. I want more than that.' A kind of defiant confidence filled her now as her eyes cleared and she saw Rocco hadn't yet run screaming from the room in horror. 'Well? Is that what you wanted to hear? Is that truthful enough for you?'

Rocco smiled now—a smile like Gracie had never seen before—and she caught a glimpse of the youth he must have once been. Her heart turned over again.

He nodded. 'Oh, yes, *cara*. That's exactly what I wanted to hear. Because, you see, I love you too—only I held back from saying it that day because I was afraid of scaring you away. I knew you had to hate me for hurting you, and I wanted to woo you slowly and methodically—until you fell so deeply in love with me that you would never leave me. But when I got home you'd gone, and all I found was your note.'

He said a long stream of words in Italian then, and Gracie touched his jaw wonderingly, finally recognising the signs of strain on his face. *For her.*

'You're talking Italian.'

Rocco grimaced. 'Since you left I haven't been able to eat, sleep or speak anything else. I had hideous curtains installed in my office and banished everyone to another floor so they couldn't witness my pain.' His face was serious. 'You brought me back to life, Gracie, and the thought of a life without you in it now terrifies me more than anything else I've ever known.'

Gracie just looked at Rocco. Her whole life flashed before her eyes. She too had always felt somehow alone... until she'd met Rocco. She'd subconsciously handed control over to him from the start, because on some level she'd already trusted him.

To her utter chagrin tears pricked her eyes again, and she cursed colourfully. 'I never used to cry until I met you.'

'That's because you finally realised you didn't have to be the strong one, the protector all the time.'

Gracie nodded as tears slipped down her cheeks and he gently caught them. 'Yes, damn you, *yes.*'

In the next second she'd thrown her arms around Rocco's neck and was in his strong embrace. Her legs were wrapped around his waist and she was sobbing into his neck. And he was crooning to her in Italian, stroking her back.

She pulled away and looked down at him. 'God, I love you, Rocco.'

He looked at her and his eyes darkened. 'I love you too, Gracie.'

He was reaching up to kiss her when she pulled back

sharply and said, 'Are you sure you're not just saying this because you still fancy me and I'm normal? What if I come back and you get tired of me and realise you really do want a society ice princess?'

Rocco looked around at the open-mouthed crowd. He felt triumph surge through him to be holding the woman he loved in his arms and to know she loved him too. *This* was the pinnacle of everything he'd ever wanted, and he'd never have known it if he hadn't met her.

He looked back to Gracie and said, 'What do you think?' He saw her take in the crowd too, and realise just what he'd done. In public. For her. Among the precious peers he'd cared about for so long.

She blushed and looked at him. 'Okay, I believe you.'

'I think it's time to go home.'

Gracie's arms were tight around his neck. 'Yes, please.'

Much later, when their bodies were finally sated and Gracie didn't know where she began and Rocco ended, she took in a deep, voluptuous sigh.

Rocco raised himself up on one arm and looked at her seriously. He brushed some hair from her cheek. 'The only reason I didn't tell you I loved you the day you left was because I didn't want to scare you with the intensity I felt. I wanted to start fresh and woo you as you deserved to be wooed.'

Gracie smiled wryly. 'I think it's safe to say you've wooed me, Rocco. I'm a sure thing.'

He reached behind him to the cabinet and got something. It was hidden in his hand as he said, 'Well, seeing as how we've fast-forwarded past the wooing stage, I'm happy to jump to the next bit.'

'The next bit?' Gracie came up on her elbow too.

Rocco was opening a small velvet box, and Gracie

looked down to see a stunning emerald ring surrounded by diamonds. She looked from it to Rocco.

He said with a glint in his eye, 'You can't take this one back to the shop. It's on loan for a lifetime.'

Gracie sat up and pulled the sheet around her. She felt shaky. Rocco took her hand and placed the ring at the top of her finger and looked into her eyes. Gracie felt tears prickle and blinked them back.

'Gracie O'Brien. I love you more than life itself. Would you come to Rio de Janeiro with me next week and become my wife, with George and Steven as our witnesses?'

Gracie nodded jerkily, tears stinging in earnest now. With a choked voice she answered, 'Yes. I'd love to come to Rio de Janeiro with you and become your wife.'

Rocco pushed the ring onto her finger and pulled her into him with a growl of triumph. Their mouths met and clung.

After a long moment Rocco pulled back and said throatily, 'Good, because then we can get to the next bit.'

'What's that?' Gracie's voice was breathless.

Sounding serious all of a sudden, he said, 'Living the rest of our lives together and having a family we can love and nurture and give everything to that we were denied.'

Feeling incredibly emotional, because she knew he was waiting to see if she wanted the same thing—which, considering their histories, was not necessarily a given— Gracie touched his cheek and said huskily, 'I'd like that. A lot.'

Four years later Gracie looked over the downy head of their newborn baby—a brother to their two-and-a-half-year-old daughter, Tessa. She smiled at her husband and said jokingly, 'Any regrets, Mr de Marco?'

Tessa shifted sleepily on his shoulder as he leant

forward to kiss Gracie tenderly. Love infused the air around them.

He pulled back after a long moment and said softly, 'Not for a second.'

* * * * *

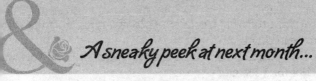

A sneaky peek at next month...

MODERN™

INTERNATIONAL AFFAIRS, SEDUCTION & PASSION GUARANTEED

My wish list for next month's titles...

In stores from 20th April 2012:

❏ A Vow of Obligation — Lynne Graham

❏ Playing the Greek's Game — Sharon Kendrick

❏ His Majesty's Mistake — Jane Porter

❏ The Darkest of Secrets — Kate Hewitt

In stores from 4th May 2012:

❏ Defying Drakon — Carole Mortimer

❏ One Night in Paradise — Maisey Yates

❏ Duty and the Beast — Trish Morey

❏ Behind the Castello Doors — Chantelle Shaw

❏ The Morning After The Wedding Before — Anne Oliver

Available at WHSmith, Tesco, Asda, Eason, Amazon and Apple

Just can't wait?

Special Offers

Every month we put together collections and longer reads written by your favourite authors.

Here are some of next month's highlights— and don't miss our fabulous discount online!

On sale 20th April

On sale 20th April

On sale 20th April

Save 20%
on all Special Releases